RIGID

SCOTT HILDRETH

Published by
Eralde Publishing

ISBN 13: 978-1544850009

DEDICATION

To all my readers, this one is for you.

But, if your name is Shannon McFarland, or Alicia Kraus, thank you for keeping me laughing, even in times of distress.

PROLOGUE

Handcuffed to the underside of a steel table and covered in a stranger's blood wasn't how I ever expected to spend a Saturday night, but it was the position I had somehow gotten myself into.

The events that got me there, however, were a blur.

A violent bloody blur that ended with one loud *boom*.

A single shot from a pistol released a bullet that tore through his flesh, pierced his skull, and killed him instantly.

I lifted my head from the cold surface of the table. My eyes aimlessly wandered around the empty room, struggling to adjust beyond the tears and confusion. I noticed cameras in the two corners of the ceiling across from me, and I was sure they were recording my every move.

The severity of what happened began to sink into my stomach like a heavy stone.

I lowered my head onto my one free arm, closed my eyes, and tried to remember exactly what happened. The scene played in my head like the trailer for a Hollywood movie, hitting only the highlights. Screaming. Blood. The sound of breaking bones. And then, a gunshot.

Bile rose in my throat. Upon reaching the back of my tongue, the vile substance caused my stomach to heave. Fearing I was going to vomit, I instinctively raised my hands to my mouth. Or, at least I tried. The metallic *clank* and a resistant jerk on my left hand stopped me short.

Once again, a reminder of what I had done.

RIGID

The door unlocked, and then swung open. A man and a woman sauntered into the room.

"I'm Detective Jones," the man said.

The woman sat down across from me. "You can call me Jacky."

Jones methodically paced the floor behind her. Each time he passed the table, the smell of stale cigarette smoke followed him. The dark skin underneath his eyes combined with his gaunt cheeks and unkempt hair made it look like he hadn't eaten or slept in a week.

He stopped pacing, turned to face me, and scratched his head feverishly with both hands. After a moment, he paused, and then met my gaze. His stare was intense, and his expression was one of disbelief.

My eyes fell to the table.

"Are you paying attention, Miss. West?"

I looked up. "Uh huh."

I didn't belong there. It shouldn't have never happened, but it did. I was sure of it. I heard the boom, and I saw the blood. I shook my head, hoping to rid my mind of my spotty recollection of what had transpired.

He shook his head lightly and shot me a condescending look. "You look like shit."

"I feel…I uhhm. I think I'm going to be sick," I murmured.

"I'd feel sick, too. I mean, shit, you just killed a guy. Blew his fucking head all over La Quinta Ave. We picked up the pieces and put 'em in a little plastic bag." He cocked an eyebrow. "How's that make you feel, being a murderer?"

My head began to spin. I struggled to recall exactly what happened, but could only resurrect the horrific portions that came in unwelcomed flashes of memory.

Jones clasped the end of the table in his hands, leaned down, and cleared his throat. "So, you pointed the gun at him, and then shouted for him to stop. You told the patrol officer on the scene that you gave that command. *Stop, or I'll shoot.*"

"Uhhm…" I tried to swallow, but my dry throat prevented it. "I don't. He was uhhm…"

"Stop or I'll shoot. That's what you said, right?"

"It was…"

"Stop or I'll shoot. You said that. *Stop or I'll shoot.* What were you prepared to do if he didn't stop, Miss West?"

Tears rolled down my cheeks. "He was…"

He slapped the table with his hand. "Stop or I'll shoot," he shouted. "You said that, right?"

I closed my eyes.

It wasn't what I'd said. I didn't say anything. Not that I could remember, anyway. I simply pulled the trigger.

"And then, when he didn't, you shot him? In the face, I might add."

I didn't remember shooting him in the face. I didn't remember shooting him at all. The last thing I could remember was yelling at him. I wanted him to stop. I needed him to stop.

But, he didn't.

"I uhhm. I think I yelled at him. I don't know," I muttered. "I'm not sure what I. I don't know."

"Stop, or I'll shoot." His eyebrows raised slightly. "And then you shot him in the face,"

"I don't." I lowered my head onto the table. The more I thought about it, the more the memories became scrambled. I looked up. "I don't remember doing that."

He pushed himself away from the table and shot me a look. "Are you suggesting that someone else shot him?"

"I don't…"

"Your fingerprints are all over the gun, Miss West. I'd love to hear a different version of the story, though." He chuckled, and then looked at Jacky. "How about you, Jacky? You want to hear how someone walked up, took the gun from her hand, shot the guy, wiped off his prints, put the gun back in her hand, and then ran away?"

Jacky extended her left arm, a silent suggestion for Jones to back away from the table. When he complied, she turned to face me and smiled. "Do you want something to drink, hun? You don't look like you're feeling well."

"I uhhm. I'd like a Sprite. Or a 7-Up. Can I have one of those?"

"Sure," she said with a nod. "I'll be right back."

She stood, looked at Jones, and then left the room. Jones paced for a moment, and then stopped directly across from me. His tired eyes met mine.

"That gun you shot him with is a pretty unique piece. Ruger SP-101. Five-shot .357 magnum with a 2" barrel. With that short barrel, they kick like a fuckin mule, huh?"

I glanced at my right hand. Amidst the dried blood, a bruise was clearly visible on my wrist. As I gazed at the discolored skin, I remembered pulling the trigger, and how much the pistol's recoil hurt.

I nodded. "Uh huh."

"So, do you remember shooting him now?"

I didn't remember shooting him, I only remembered the *boom* and the blinding flash of light.

I looked at him. My eyes felt itchy. "I uhhm."

The door opened, and Jacky walked in. After sitting down across from me, she poured some soda in a cup and slid it across the table. "Have a drink, it'll make you feel better."

Jones tossed a yellow notepad and a pen beside me. "While you're sipping that soda, why don't you write down what happened? Every detail. How you told him to stop, and then how you shot him. I'd get him to write it down, but he's in the morgue. His family's going to be planning his funeral, Miss. West. You telling the truth will help them put this to rest. That makes sense, doesn't it?"

It didn't.

The guy was a piece of shit. I did the world – and his family – a favor. It may sound harsh, but it was the truth.

I took a sip of soda, and glanced at the notepad. After another drink, I reached for the pen. I closed my eyes and tried to recall exactly what happened. The sound of the door unlocking caused me to look up.

A handsome man who was wearing slacks and a dress blazer walked in.

Jacky stood and gave a sharp nod toward the man. "Detective Watson."

Jones looked nervous. He extended his hand. "Watson."

Watson looked at Jones, didn't shake his hand, and then shot a quick glance at me. He nodded his head once as if affirming my presence and then turned toward the two outwardly nervous detectives.

He cleared his throat. "Jones. Trovetti. I'll be taking this investigation over."

"Hold up," Jones said. "This is our murder collar. You're not going to--"

"Yes, I am." Watson reached for the chair Jacky had been sitting in, and then paused. "If you've got a problem with it, talk to the commissioner."

Jones' eyes widened. "The commissioner?"

Watson motioned toward the door. "Close that on your way out, would you?"

Jones pressed his hands against his hips and blinked a few times. "The commissioner?"

Watson nodded. "Yeah, the commissioner. Remember him? He's a tall fucker with thick curly hair and an addiction to sunflower seeds. His office is at the end of the hallway on the seventh floor. He's got a plaque on the door in case you get confused on which office is his." He tilted his head toward the door. "Go ask him, but don't forget to get the door on the way out."

Jacky and Jones exchanged an awkward glance, and then left the room.

Watson sat across from me, leaned forward, and looked me in the eyes. He didn't smell like stale cigarettes or resemble the walking dead. The air around him smelled like expensive cologne, and he looked like an athlete.

He held my gaze, cupped his hands around his mouth, and then looked down at the table. I wondered if he was mad, or if he was thinking or praying. Then, he spoke.

Well, kind of.

"Say *I want an attorney present*, and say it loudly," he whispered.

What he said was almost inaudible, but I understood him.

I blinked my eyes in disbelief.

"Say it," he whispered.

I wondered why he was helping me, but didn't dare ask. I looked at the camera, cleared my throat, and made the declaration.

"I want an attorney present."

He looked up. His eyebrow arched. "Excuse me?"

"I want an…I want to have an attorney present."

"If that's how you want to play this." He pushed himself away from the table and stood. "Fine. I'll take you to the phone."

He uncuffed me and motioned toward the door. "Second door on your right. I'll follow you, it's procedure."

I walked down the hall, and into a much larger room than the one I had been in. A wooden table surrounded by chairs was in the center of the room, and at the edge of the table, a phone sat.

Watson pulled the door closed behind him. "This is a private room. What you say here isn't recorded. You're not going to call an attorney."

Even more confused than I was before, I stared back at him, blankly.

He met my muddled gaze. "You're going to call Alexandra."

"Lex?"

He nodded. "Tell her you've been arrested for murder, and that you need *Jay Parsons.*"

I had no idea what he was talking about. He just as well had spoke to me in Italian. It would have made an equal amount of sense. My wide-eyed stare must have prompted him to explain further, because that's what he did.

"*Lex, I've been arrested on a murder charge, and I need you to call Jay Parsons. They want to interrogate me, and I need an attorney.* That's what you'll say," he said. "No more, no less. Understand?"

"Okay."

The look on his face changed to concern. "Are you alright?"

"I'll be…yeah. I'm uhhm. I'm fine." I nodded, more to convince myself than to reassure him. "Is she uhhm…"

A flash of memory came to mind, and it wasn't something I ever wanted to see again. Panic shot up my throat, choking me from continuing. I fought against it, wiped my tears, and looked up. I needed to know. "She didn't uhhm. Is she alive?"

He reached for my shoulder and gave a nod of reassurance. "I just left the hospital. She's alive, yes."

"She's not going to die?"

"She'll recover fully. That's what the doctor said, I can promise you that."

Emotion washed over me, and I blubbered for an instant. After regaining what little composure I could, I wiped my eyes with the heels of my palms. "Thank you."

He released my shoulder. "I'm going to leave the room, and as soon as I do, you need to make that call."

"But, she's okay? Right?"

"She looks like hell, but I promise you, she'll be okay."

"Why. Why uhhm. Why are you helping me?"

"Because you've got something I need," he said.

Then, he turned around and left the room.

ONE

Sandy

Lex and I were best friends and co-workers. Her boyfriend, Cholo, was a fully patched member of a local Motorcycle Club, the Filthy Fuckers. Contrary to popular opinions about bikers, he was kind, sweet, protective, and loyal. Considering her success with him – and my lack of success with men in general – I decided to meet a friend of his, another patched member of the club.

With a bucket of iced Budweiser at my side and my chair pointed toward the front door, I eagerly waited for them to show up. When they finally walked in, I stared in disbelief.

Hell, anyone would have.

My potential date was handsome, outwardly cocky, and had the muscular structure of a running back. Short of the kutte he wore, he looked like he could be a tattooed model for a clothing company.

"Oh. My. God." I picked my jaw up from my lap and rapped my knuckles against the table. "Is *that* him?"

Lex glanced over her shoulder and then looked at me. "Yep."

Cholo nudged his buddy and motioned toward where we were sitting. As they walked in our direction, I couldn't help but notice my date's undeniable swagger. Confidence radiated from him, and he didn't have to speak for me to realize it.

He wore it like a crown.

I pried my eyes from his handsome face and gave Lex a quick look.

13

"Is he an asshole?"

"No. He's just. I don't know." She shrugged one shoulder. "Intense."

"Intense?" My eyes darted back and forth between him and her. "Like, in a good way?"

Her mouth twisted to the side. "Uhhm…"

It didn't matter. I'd already made up my mind. With looks like that, he could be a little bit of an asshole, and I'd somehow find a way to accept it.

He stopped at the edge of the table and looked me up and down. He raked his fingers through his closely cropped hair, and then hooked his thumbs on the edges of his front pockets.

His blue eyes met mine. "You Sandy?"

I opened my mouth to speak, but my throat had gone tight, leaving me no alternative but to nod.

After taking another quick look at me, he took a step back. He tilted his head toward the door. "C'mon."

I shot him a deer in the headlights look. Somehow, I managed to speak. Kind of. "Huh?"

He did the head toward the door thing again. "C'mon, we're leaving."

"We're uhhm..." I stammered.

He hadn't even introduced himself. I looked at Lex. She shrugged. I looked up and blinked a few times. "Leaving?"

His eyes fell to my boobs. He grinned and coughed his response. "Yeah."

I had just finished my period, and I was horny as hell, but I wasn't an easy lay. I was pretty sure I'd let him fuck me at some point, but it wasn't going to happen until I wanted it to. Hot biker or not, he was going to have to wait until *I* was ready.

"I'm not going anywhere," I said adamantly. "Not yet, anyway. You haven't even introduced yourself. Sit down."

He pursed his lips, looked me over, and then grabbed the seat beside me. After turning it around backward, he sat and draped his arms over the chair's back. I glanced at his full sleeve of tattoos, but made it a point not to stare.

A colorful array of dragons, flowers, and skulls covered his right arm all the way down to his hand.

Interesting.

He cleared his throat. "Name's Smoke."

"Smoke?" I chuckled. "That's your name?"

He nodded. "Yep."

"Mine's Fire," I said with a laugh.

He didn't seem amused. I wrestled the smile from my face and changed my tone to serious. "Seriously, what's your name?"

"Smoke," he said flatly.

"Okay." I nodded and extended my hand. "I'm Sandy. Nice to meet you, Smoke."

He shook my hand and gave a slight grin. "Ditto."

His sexy appearance and handsome looks had my interest. The jury, however, was still out on him. As I stared back at him and tried to decide what to talk about, I wondered just where he thought we were going to go had I chosen to get up and leave when he asked me.

He tilted his head toward the bucket of beers. "You mind?"

"No, we ordered them for you guys."

"Appreciate ya." He pulled a bottle from the bucket, handed it to Cholo, and then grabbed another. After opening it, he drank half the bottle in one gulp.

"So, what do you two want to do?" Lex asked.

I shifted my eyes from him to her and shrugged. "I don't care."

I really didn't. The excitement of meeting someone new had taken over, and whatever we chose to do would satisfy me.

"We could go for a ride," Cholo said.

"We're headed out in a minute," Smoke said.

I looked at him. He was leaning over the back of the chair with the bottle of beer, which was now empty, dangling loosely from his fingertips.

Oh really?

"Relax," I said. "Have another beer."

He set the bottle aside and shook his head. "I don't ride drunk. One's my limit."

I looked at Cholo, expecting him to laugh or say something contradictory. He grinned and nodded. "He never drinks more than one."

I shifted my eyes to Smoke. He shrugged and then stood. "You about ready?"

The thought of leaving with him excited me, but I wanted to act indifferent. "Where are we going to go?"

"We'll head to Belmont Park, get some ice cream, and then maybe take a walk along Mission Beach. Toes in the sand sound good?"

Holy crap.

A handsome biker who had so much confidence it oozed from his pores, and he was romantic.

Who was I to argue?

I grabbed my purse, stood, and then met his gaze. "Really?"

He leaned toward me, brushed my hair to the side, and then pressed his mouth to my ear. "No," he whispered, forcing his warm breath into my ear. "We're going to your place, get to know each other a little, and see what happens. Now, turn around, wave at your friends, and smile."

Goosebumps raised along the biceps of both my arms. The thought of having sex with him was exciting, but I wasn't a whore, and I didn't want him to expect that sex was a sure thing.

"I'm not a whore," I whispered.

"Didn't say you were. We're both adults, though. And, I think you're hot as fuck." His hand slid along my side and stopped at the small of my back. "You gonna wave at 'em, or not?"

I turned around, swallowed hard, and forced a grin. "We're uhhm. We're going to go ahead and go."

Lex's eyes slowly widened. Her smirk returned. She must have known. Cholo pinched the bill of his cap in a biker 'goodbye' wave.

I shot him a nervous smile and turned around.

Now facing the door with my blind date at my side, I was anxious and excited at the same time.

"Uhhm. Tell me a little about yourself," I said, hoping to rid myself of the apprehension that filled me.

"I'll tell you *everything* about me." He chuckled and then began walking toward the door. "I like riding, eating at shitty diners, drinking coffee, and fucking."

At least he was honest.

He pushed the front door open, mean-mugged a man as he walked past us, and then motioned for me to walk though. I stepped onto the sidewalk, and turned to face him. I wanted to act like he hadn't shocked me, even though he had.

"Your list. Are they in order?" I asked. "From favorite to least favorite?"

He reached for the back of my neck, gripped it lightly in his hand, and pulled me close to his chest. His eyes met mine, and he held my gaze for an instant. I struggled to swallow as he leaned forward, brushing his cheek against mine as he did so.

"That depends on how good you are at fucking," he breathed into my ear.

Dear fucking God.

It was too much.

My eyes fell closed and my legs went weak.

He lowered his hand, leaned away, and gave me a look.

I don't know if he was trying to drive me insane or not, but he was doing a good job of it. I stood in place, incapable of doing much else. With a wet pussy and a wandering mind, I tried to come up with one good reason *not* to fuck him.

I produced nothing, good or bad. Convinced that was the direction the night was going to go, my curious side presented itself.

"Why are we going to my house?" I asked.

"My daughter is at my place, and I don't make it a point of bringing women around her. In fact, I've got a rigid policy against it."

His response wasn't at all what I was expecting. My mind instantly went to thoughts of him being married, and that he was a typical cheating douche.

"Are you married?"

He shot me a look. "If I was, I wouldn't be here, would I?"

I felt like somewhat of a fool for asking, but not a complete fool. Men cheated, it was a fact of life. I'd been the recipient of some of it in the past, and I wasn't interested in having it happen again.

"Guys cheat," I said with a shrug. "I just thought--"

"Well, I don't. Never have, never will."

Hearing it was reassuring, but I couldn't help but wonder about him being single, and about the child.

"So, you're single?"

He motioned toward his Harley. "What did I just say?"

He took a few steps, and then paused when I didn't immediately follow him. As he glanced over his shoulder, my curious side reared its ugly head again.

"Who's watching your daughter?"

"Jesus with the questions," he said with a laugh. "She watches herself."

"What?" I snapped. "You can't leave a child at home alone--"

He arched an eyebrow. "Listen, *Sandy*. I've been a single father from the day after she was born until now, and she's seventeen fucking years old. I'd really appreciate it if you don't tell me what I can and can't do with her, because considering all things, I've done a good God damned job of bringing her up. I'm pretty fucking proud of her, and of the job I've done."

I swallowed hard. "Seventeen? You don't look like you're old enough to--"

"She's sixteen. She'll be seventeen here real quick. And, I'm thirty-four. I started young." He reached for the helmet that dangled from his handlebars. "We doing this deal, or not?"

What little reservation I had about taking him home vanished after his speech about his daughter. I was right back where I'd started, only now I saw him as a handsome biker *and* a hot single dad.

"You got another helmet?"

"You ask a lot of fucking questions."

19

I shrugged. "I'm a girl."

He opened the compartment on the back of his motorcycle, pulled out a helmet, and handed it to me. "Yeah, every time you open your mouth, you remind me of that."

"I'll try and keep my mouth shut, then," I said, my voice thick with sarcasm.

"That's fine with me," he said with a laugh. "I'll let you know when it's time for you to open it."

I raised my index finger. "Oh, one last thing."

He widened his eyes and cocked his head to the side.

"Can we stop at CVS?"

His brow wrinkled. "What?"

"I need to get protection," I whispered. "In case we uhhm--"

"I've been clipped," he said.

"Huh?"

He pointed at his crotch and then made the scissor finger gesture. "Vasectomy. I've had a vasectomy."

I stole a quick look at him while he flipped switches and made adjustments. He was as handsome of a man as I had ever seen, and his confidence made him seem even more so. Feeling compelled to make my point, I pried my eyes away from his cute butt and cleared my throat.

"I'm on the pill, but that doesn't mean we do it without protection. *If* we do it. I'm not saying we will, because we probably won't. Not tonight. But, if it ends up that we do, I just think--"

He started the motorcycle when I was mid-sentence and began revving the engine. The high-pitched sound of the exhaust was impossible to speak over.

I couldn't decide if he was an asshole, or just acted like one. Either way, I guessed, would produce the same result.

I could forego the asshole in him for one night.

And, regardless of what he said or I thought, I was sure that was as far as it would go.

TWO

Smokey

After passing eighteen of her twenty *get to know me* questions, we sat around and shot the shit for an hour and a half. As much as normally hated the question-answer bullshit, I enjoyed our talk immensely. Then, about the time I was ready to call it a night and ride off into the sunset, she reminded me of my earlier offer to fuck her.

I'd never been one to deny a woman of her carnal desires, and I wasn't about to start with Sandy.

We'd been fucking on and off for over an hour, and she'd reached a point that she could barely stand. Naked, and leaning against the kitchen island with a bottle of water in her hand, she gazed down at the floor and struggled to catch her breath.

Standing on the other side of the counter, I admired her body, long blonde hair, and ability to take a stiff cock like a paid professional. Most women would have begged me to stop after thirty minutes. Her willingness – and ability – to go an hour without complaint was pretty god damned impressive.

After several short choppy breaths, she looked up. "So…is this… what you…do?"

"No," I said matter-of-factly, struggling to keep a straight face. "I normally don't take breaks. But you looked like you were gonna have a fucking heart attack."

She coughed out a laugh. "No...I meant..." She paused, looked at the ceiling, and then met my gaze. "Jesus...I can't...I meant...*the fucking.* Is this normal?"

Typically, I didn't get confused about anything, but she was doing a good job of changing that.

I looked her up one side and down the other. "What in the fuck are you talking about?"

"Do you always fuck like *this*?"

I wrinkled my nose and stared. "Like what?"

She shrugged. "Hard?"

"I only fuck one way." I said. "If you don't like it..."

"No." She grinned. "I like it. A lot."

I'd given her every inch of dick I owned, and I'd given it to her pretty good. If she was smiling afterward, we were far from done. I needed her to fully understand just what it was that I'd expect of her if she decided to give me another whirl sometime.

"Good." I stepped back and stroked my cock a few times. "You ready?"

Her eyes fell to my crotch, stared for a moment, and then raised slowly. "For?"

I thought I'd made myself clear. Obviously not. I shook my head in disbelief and chuckled out a light laugh. "To start fucking again, what else?"

"Is this..." She set the bottle of water on the counter. "Is this a one-night stand?"

"I think you're cool as fuck. But, I already told you, I don't do relationships," I said with a slight shrug. "Whether we see each other again or not depends on you, not me."

She was a beautiful woman, there was no denying it. Her quick-witted personality only added to her attractiveness. If I was going to be in a relationship, she was the type of girl I would want to be with, but doing so – at least now – wasn't an option.

And, by the time I was ready, she'd be like all the rest.

Long gone.

"I'm getting bored," she said. "Are you going to fuck me or stand there with your cock in your hand?"

If nothing else, she was eager. I liked that she had enough confidence to talk shit, too. Her willingness to do everything I'd asked of her was impressive, but I needed to make sure she didn't *like* me.

She could like fucking me, but that's where the attraction needed to stop.

Determined to find her breaking point, I gestured toward her living room. "C'mon, smart ass. I'm losing my wood."

She walked past me and into the living room, then paused.

Standing fifteen feet or so in front of me, and naked as fuck, she turned toward me and grinned. Her olive-colored skin, athletic body, and cute as hell face were enough to make any man want to fuck her.

Compelled to admire her perfect body, I stood and stared for a moment. She batted her eyelashes, squeezed her boobs together with her biceps, and smiled. The gesture drew me to her like a sexual vacuum.

My twitching cock reminded me to stop admiring and start fucking.

Her eyes fell to my crotch. "Oh. Wow."

I wanted her to hate me, so I responded in a typical Smokey-ism. "Bend over the couch and finger your twat."

I wasn't naturally a prick. To be honest, I had to try pretty hard to

25

accomplish the task. Having her finger her twat wasn't something I wanted her to do, or anything that I particularly wanted to see. I told her to do it to make her think I was an asshole.

Having her feel that way about me would keep her at arm's length and preserve my relationship with my daughter.

She didn't ague or ask questions, she simply smiled, bent over, and stuck her finger in her sexy bald pussy. It was becoming painfully obvious if I wasn't a single father, that she'd make the short list of women that I was attracted to.

Bent over with her chest flat against the couch, she fingered her pussy with one hand while she rubbed her clit with the other. Instantly, I went from not wanting to see it to becoming immersed in the sight.

After fingering herself into an audible lather, she added another finger.

It may have been her moaning that excited me initially, but watching her finger-bang herself with two delicate digits while she whacked away at her swollen clit with her other hand had my cock bouncing up and down like it used to in my teen years.

Her moans of pleasure combined with the sight of her picture-perfect pussy were too much. I tore my eyes away from her beautiful display of self-pleasure, and cleared my throat.

"Turn around and suck my cock," I said with a tone of authority.

In my tenure as a biker, I'd been with all types. The willing, the not so willing, the talented, and the turds. I'd fucked the experienced, and given a little dick to a handful of virgins. Across the board, it was a fifty-fifty mix of those who were eager to suck a cock, and those who weren't.

She stood, turned around, and dropped to her knees like a giraffe that'd been shot with a tranquilizer dart.

I guided my cock into her open mouth. "Impress me."

And, impress me she did. Without hesitation, she took half my cock into her mouth. My eyes went wide at the sight of it. Half of it was equal to most men's entire shaft.

With her mouth stretched wide, and her tongue pressed against the bottom side of my cock, she paused, looked up at me, and winked.

So far, the night had been limited to me fucking her doggy style in front if the couch, her riding my cock while I played with her tits, and me spending a few minutes with my cock between her massive jugs.

This was her chance to shine.

And so far, she was doing just that. If nothing else, I'd give her a point for the wink.

She forced my cock into the back of her throat, gagged until her eyes watered, and then pulled her mouth free. After giving the head of my dick a glare that would have scared most young children to tears, she licked a dangling droplet from the tip, and then attacked it like a wolf going after a dying sheep.

Her head bobbed like it was on a swivel. Drool ran down her chin and onto my nuts with each attempt at shoving it down her throat. I watched her until I was afraid I was going to blow a nut down her warm and willing throat, and then I pressed my hand against her forehead.

I couldn't take it any longer. She was far too good at giving head, and I wasn't about to have her feel like she'd outfucked me.

But it was pretty fucking obvious she could.

In fact, it was quite possible I'd found me a ringer.

"Time to switch it up." I pulled my cock from her mouth. "Bend over the couch."

She wiped her mouth on the back of her hand. "You didn't like it?"

She sucked a cock like she'd invented the art. I wasn't about to tell her, though. Mentally, I added another point for her eager attitude.

"It was alright," I lied. I motioned toward the couch. "Bend over."

Upon hearing my request, she bent over the front of the couch and hiked her ass high in the air.

Her little swollen puss was as pretty as any I'd ever seen. Glistening from her juices, and opened up like a Valentine's Day rose, it was begging for me to enjoy it.

I guided the tip of my stiff dick toward her slit, parted her wet lips, and then pushed half my length inside of her in one heavy shove.

The air shot from her lungs like a ball from a civil war cannon.

Her pussy felt like heaven. I could easily get lost in fucking her, but I wasn't about to allow myself to do so, or tell her how much I enjoyed it.

"Put your chest down flat on the couch," I said in a demanding tone.

She gulped a breath and complied.

I gave a mental nod of appreciation, and then kicked my foot against the inside arch of her feet. "Spread em wide."

Again, she complied.

With her legs spread wide, she stood there with a twat filled with cock and her chest plastered to the edge of the couch cushion.

I lifted my right leg, planted my heel against the back of the couch, and pushed forward with my hips. The maneuver extended my leg until it was almost straight, and in turn, shoved what little cock I had left deep inside her.

She let out a moan like she was being impaled.

In most respects, she was.

I gazed down between the cheeks of her little round ass. My cock was so deep in her that my balls were smashed into her wet folds.

Fucking her was different than what I'd become accustomed to. Even after telling her that I wouldn't be willing to entertain a relationship with her, she had agreed to have sex. Most women who did the same thing were worried about one thing and one thing only.

Getting off.

She, on the other hand, had already experienced no less than half a dozen orgasms, and seemed to be more interested in getting me off than anything else.

"That's every inch of dick I own," I announced. I twisted my left foot back and forth in the carpet, made sure I was on stable ground, and then slid my thumb between her ass cheeks.

I cleared my throat. "You ready to fuck a little bit?"

A muffled grunt came from the couch cushions.

I planned on fucking her a lot, but I wasn't going to get caught up in lexical semantics.

I slowly pulled the entire length of my cock from inside of her, enjoying watching it slide free of her tight cunt. As the tip cleared her pussy lips, she let out a sigh.

My glistening cock danced between her ass cheeks.

I grinned and gave a slight nod, reassuring myself I was ready for action. After sliding my thumb along her ass crack and pressing it deep into her wet twat, I grabbed my juice-covered shaft in my other hand.

After a few deep pumps of my thumb into her pussy, I pulled it out and slowly pushed it inside her tight ass.

Her body heaved up and down as she took a breath and then exhaled.

I guided my cock between her legs, and upon entering her warmth, shoved it balls deep.

She moaned in pleasure, and then grunted when it bottomed out, but not one time did she bitch or complain. After twenty solid minutes of a consecutive thumb and pussy fucking, and I was so fucking excited about her tight little twat that I was on the verge of blowing my nut.

But, I needed her tight little pussy first.

I pulled my thumb from her ass, grabbed her hips firmly in my hands, and continued my balls-deep assault of her glorious little cunt.

The sound of my hips slapping against her tight ass wasn't enough to drown out her moans of pleasure. Hearing her express the satisfaction I provided was music to my ears.

My balls tightened, warning me of their need to release.

I pushed her forward, pulled my cock from inside of her, and lifted my right foot from the couch.

I clenched my cock in my fist. "On your knees."

She dropped to her knees in front of me and opened her mouth.

I stroked my cock a few times and arched my back. I didn't need to see what was happening, I'd watched myself come on the faces of countless club whores and groupies. As I fisted my cock like an 80's porn star, I felt my balls pulse repeatedly, draining me of my sacred juice.

After groaning out a satisfying war cry, I looked down, eager to see my accomplishment.

Not a trace of cum was to be found.

Mystified, I stared at her with my mouth agape. If asked, I would have claimed I'd shot an award-winning load onto her mug.

She stood, almost falling in the process. I steadied her and then stared in amazement.

I gave her three points for the disappearing cum trick. Any girl that could eat that much cum was a trooper.

She flipped her hair over her shoulder and stretched her neck from side to side. "Are you done?"

"Yep," I said. "The show's over."

"Okay." She motioned toward the door. "You can leave now."

My eyes went wide. "Excuse me?"

"This is my house. You don't do relationships, and we're done fucking. So, there's not much left for us to do." She waved her hand back and forth like she was a mechanical mannequin at the entrance of a carnival. "Bye."

I chuckled at her strength. I wouldn't have guessed it. At least not initially.

"You're kicking me out?"

"I'm kindly asking you to leave. You're a great lay, for what it's worth. I came *really* hard that time. Thank you. You've got a nice cock, by the way."

As she cleaned up, I got dressed and laced up my boots. At the instant she walked out of the bathroom, I pulled on my kutte.

Still quite shocked at what had happened, I grinned, waved, and sauntered toward the door. Halfway there, I turned around.

"We gonna see each other again?"

"Maybe," she said. "I'll let you know."

I admired her independent strength, eager attitude, gorgeous smile, and ability to understand my awkward needs. I hated that I had to be the way I was, but there was just no other way for me to protect the love of my life.

Eddie.

THREE

Sandy

Lex and I sat in the Crab Shack for our afternoon drink, but she wasn't drinking. She was giddy about the news, and although I was happy for her, I couldn't imagine how I'd react if the same thing happened to me. I guess I could imagine it, I simply couldn't imagine being happy about it.

I took a drink of my beer and shook my head. "I still can't believe it," I said. "It just happened like *that*."

She looked at me like I was an idiot. "Isn't that how it always happens? It isn't like it normally creeps up on you. You either are, or you're not."

"Yeah, I guess you're right."

"I didn't want to say anything until I knew, though."

"When you said that you didn't feel like drinking the other day, I knew something was going on."

"I wanted to make sure." She shrugged. "Now, I know."

I wagged my eyebrows as I took another drink of my beer.

Lex was pregnant, and although she and her boyfriend weren't married, they were living together. From what she said, he was as excited as she was for the baby. Their relationship was one that would be easy for anyone to envy, because Cholo was the type of man that every girl wanted.

He was handsome, kind, considerate, loving, and uncomplicated. He

33

put it all out there, and left nothing to the imagination. In my mind, it was a huge plus.

I pushed my empty bottle of beer to the side. "So, what did the doctor say?"

"Other than I'm pregnant? Nothing, really. They don't tell you much. She gave me a bunch of literature to read. Oh, and she suggested some books."

"I hate doctors. They're like attorneys. Overpaid."

She laughed. "Unless you need one."

"I'm not planning on needing either."

"How'd the deal go with Smoke? He's pretty in-your-face, isn't he?"

I let out a laugh, even though I didn't really mean to. She looked at me as if she wanted an explanation for my outburst, but I tried to dismiss our night together as uneventful.

I shifted my focus to the table. "It went good."

"What? Why'd you laugh?"

I looked up. "I don't know."

She leaned back and looked at me. "You guys did it, didn't you?"

Lex wasn't a prude by any means, but she wasn't one to have sex with random guys, that was for sure. She and Cholo were together for several months before they had sex. Even then, their relationship was rock solid before she committed to do it with him.

I knew she wouldn't judge me, but I was still reluctant to tell her the complete truth. I decided to give her part of it, and then try to divert her attention somewhere else.

"We went back to my place, talked for a while, and hung out. Did you know he has a daughter?"

Her eyes shot wide. "Wait. What? Seriously?"

I nodded. "Almost seventeen years old. He's a single father."

She shook her head. "I had no idea."

"Well, he is. I don't know, maybe don't tell Cholo about it. If he hasn't told you, he might not know. Smoke didn't say not to tell you, but it just seems kind of weird that you don't know."

"You know how those guys are, they're secretive. They don't tell anyone anything."

"What do you mean?"

"They don't say much about anything, and they say a lot less about each other," she said. "It's probably an oath of silence or something."

I shot her a look. "Really?"

"I don't know. I was kidding. Kind of. I'm sure they don't take an oath, they're just secretive."

"Well, he's got a daughter. Says he can't be in a relationship because of her."

"What?" She snapped back. "That sounds like bullshit. Wouldn't you want to be in a relationship if you were a single father?"

I twisted my mouth to the side and shrugged one shoulder. "I don't know. He said he was protecting her from being hurt. It made sense."

She looked at me like my head was on fire. "Being hurt?"

"That's what he said. He told me about his daughter's mother, and how she left after the baby was born. He said he wasn't going to give another woman a chance to hurt her again."

Her eyes slowly widened. "Oh wow. She left right after the baby was born?"

"He said she left right after, yeah. Like maybe even a few days after, I don't know. But not like after a month or anything, it was early. He took off work for six months to bottle feed her. Then he fired the first nanny he hired after the first day. He said he was doing construction work, and he started taking her to work with him. Kept it up until kindergarten."

"Holy crap," she gasped. "I had no idea. That's impressive. I mean, it sucks that he won't be in a relationship, but I understand the position he's taking."

"I kind of felt sorry for him."

She shook her head lightly, and then looked at me. "You did it with him, didn't you?"

I was out of ammunition to divert her attention. I wondered if she'd think less of me, and then decided she wouldn't.

I let out a sigh. "Yeah."

"You skank." She chuckled. "I knew you would."

"It's not being a skank if I'm in control of when, where, and how. I needed it," I said. "And I really enjoyed it."

"Your dick fix?"

I chuckled. "Uh huh."

"So, what now?"

I shrugged. "That's it. We had sex."

"You're okay with that?"

"Yeah. We used each other. I was horny, he was horny. We used each other. I kicked him out when we were done."

"What do you mean?"

"As soon as we were done, I asked him to leave."

"Oh wow." She took a drink of her tea, and then looked up. "He didn't ask you to give him a lap dance or anything, did he?"

I worked with Lex at the seafood restaurant during the day, and worked nights at the local strip club. I'd been contemplating quitting, but the amount of money I made was difficult to walk away from.

"I didn't tell him I danced. Did you?"

"No, I didn't tell him. Did you quit the club already?" she asked.

"Not yet."

"Are you going to?"

"I haven't decided."

"Is all Smokey's worried about is protecting his daughter from meeting someone? I mean, is he willing to like, *go out* as long as that's all it is?"

I wondered about how we left things, and if he'd be receptive to such a suggestion. If it included sex, I was sure he'd see value in it.

The thought of fucking him again bothered me. Not because I wouldn't enjoy it, because I knew I would. My problem was that I feared I'd want it over, and over.

"I don't know," I said. "I think so."

"Figure out when your next night off is, and then why don't you ask him. Maybe we could all do something together."

I knew I'd have to make the promise of sex to even think about luring him into a night out with another couple. The thought of doing so wasn't as exciting as it should be. Maybe it was because I wasn't sure how long I'd be able to continue fucking him without developing feelings.

After struggling with it for a moment, I decided I could fuck him one more time and walk away safely.

I gave her a look of reassurance and grinned at the thought of it. "I think I can talk him into it."

FOUR

Smokey

Contentious matters seemed to be handled in the kitchen, and that's where we were. I stood on one side of the island, and she on the other. It was a good thing there was something separating us, because she looked like she wanted to choke me.

"We've been over this and over this for the last year," I said. "You know damned good and well that I'm not going to change my mind. You've got another month, and then I'll agree to it. Now, I won't."

She pressed her hands to her hips and glared at me. "He's not going to wait a month. He'll find someone else to take out."

"Then he'll find someone else."

She shot me a sideways glare. "You don't care?"

Upsetting her was the last thing on earth I wanted to do. It hurt me to see her upset, but it would hurt me much worse to see a boy take advantage of her. I wanted to prolong her single status for as long as possible, and the rule of our home was no dating until she was seventeen.

"It's not that I don't care, because I do," I explained. "I want you to be happy, but I don't want you to get hurt. The rule is you can date when you're seventeen. Not sixteen. Not sixteen and a half, and not sixteen and eleven months. Seventeen. That's the rule."

She tossed her hands in the air. "A rule you made up."

39

"All rules are made up."

She let out a long sigh, rolled her eyes, and then looked at me. "I want to go on the record as saying that this is the stupidest and most sadistic rule you've ever conjured up."

"On the record?" I coughed out a laugh. "You're not in a court of law."

"Just as well be. You keep notes. So, keep that one. The stupidest and most sadistic."

"I don't keep notes."

"Really? Now I'm stupid, huh?" She shook her head. "You're brain's a vault. You keep mental notes. You always have. And you forget *nothing*."

She was right. I did make mental notes, and I rarely forgot anything. I held grudges, too.

"Stupid and sadistic," I said. "Duly noted."

She glared at me playfully.

The thought of my daughter going on a date made me cringe. I didn't care who the guy was, he wasn't going to be good enough for me. I didn't want her to grow up, and her going on dates was the last step in her becoming a woman.

"What's sadistic about it?" I asked.

She arched an eyebrow. "Seriously?"

I nodded and waited for her response. She twisted her mouth to the side, undoubtedly preparing the verbal assault she was going to unleash on me. When she had time to think, she often gave well thought out responses that were indicative of her intelligence, and her odd system of beliefs.

I mentally exhaled, then reached into my pocket and pulled out my vape. After taking a long pull on it, I waited for her barrage of words.

She cleared her throat and shot me her signature stink-eye look. "Hell-o. Are you in the house, or outside?"

I lowered my vape and raised my eyebrows.

She nodded her head toward my hand. "Do we smoke that ridiculous thing in the house when I'm home?"

My lungs were filled with 10 cubic feet of 440-degree lemon flavored water vapor. I needed to exhale, but didn't dare. Not in the house, anyway.

With my lungs burning and my cheeks puffed out, I shook my head. I'm sure I looked like a teen who had been caught smoking weed by his parents.

She pointed toward the door. "Outside."

I raised my index finger.

"You have your rules, and I have mine," she snarled. "Out. Side."

After blowing the cloud of smoke out the front door, I turned to face her. "I forgot you were here."

"That's how important I've become? I'm transparent?"

"No, it's not--"

"Me and my needs? We're see through? Invisible Eddie"

"You know damned good and well that there's no one on this earth that's more important to me than you. It's a habit. I'm getting better."

"If you won't let me smoke one, you shouldn't smoke one around me."

"Law says eighteen to smoke one, so it's eighteen to smoke one."

She twisted her hair with her index finger. "Everyone at school has one."

"Maybe they've got shit parents."

RIGID

"Yeah. I'm sure that's the case. Anyway. Sadistic. Here's why it's sadistic." She leaned forward, rested her forearms on the edge of the countertop, and locked eyes with me. "A woman wants reassurance that she's beautiful. She wants…no strike that. She *needs* to feel that she's been accepted by the person or persons she seeks affirmation from. That confirmation, that reassurance, when it comes? It builds self-esteem. Now, we both know I'm not one of those girls that has low self-esteem, but a little boost from time to time sure doesn't hurt. Conversely, when a woman doesn't get said reassurance of her beauty? It whittles away at the fiber of her being. In time, she becomes downtrodden and oppressed. Then, by the time she's, I don't know, say 23 or 24, she's an easy mark for anyone who will give her a moment's notice. Your knowledge of my need for said reassurance, and lack of willingness to provide it, is nothing short of sadistic. It leaves me to wonder if you actually enjoy seeing my self-esteem pummeled into a pile of mush."

"Really?" I cocked an eyebrow. "A pile of mush?"

"Like wet sawdust. Or, remember when we went to Georgia to see your brother? The grits? Remember the grits?"

I nodded.

"That bowl of grits." She leaned back and gave a quick nod. "That's going to be my self-esteem if this keeps up."

"And going on a date with Jonny the football player will fix that?"

"His name's Richard."

"You want to go on a date with a guy named Dick?"

She let out an exaggerated sigh. "Richard."

Eddie had more self-esteem than any other 16-year-old girl on earth. She was beautiful, and to keep her reminded of it, I made it a point to tell her every day. She inherited my height, and stood almost 5'-10". Tall and lean, her blue eyes and well-developed chest set her apart from the masses at school.

But.

They were a magnet for the testosterone-filled teenage boys.

"Richard, Dick, Jonny, Frank, Pete. It doesn't matter. Tell him you'll go out with him. Just set the date a month from now. Hell, tell him your schedule is booked up until then."

"That's a ridiculous idea."

"It's a great idea."

She shook her head. "Have you always been this way?"

"What way?"

"Sadistic?"

I grinned. "Most of my life, yeah."

She scanned me from head to toe, and then looked me in the eyes. "Figures."

The timer on the stove beeped, saving me from further criticism.

"Go wash your hands," she said. "It'll be ready in a minute."

"I washed them when I got home from--"

She shot me her signature stink eye, a side-eyed glare. "You've been handling that nasty vape thing, and who knows where else your hands have been. Wash 'em."

"Love you, Ed."

As she opened the oven door, she glanced over her shoulder. "I love you, too, you sadistic jerk."

FIVE

Sandy

In hindsight, I realized I should have never agreed to it. I was really enjoying our night out – it was riding on the motorcycle that I should have refused to do.

Smoke agreed to go on a date with Cholo and Lex. The men, of course, insisted that we ride on the motorcycles. I didn't object, but I later realized I should have. With his club brother riding at his side, he was comfortable, and he was *different*.

He was fun, funny, had a more machismo demeanor, and seeing the differences made him far more attractive. I wanted to despise him for being the way he was about relationships, but I couldn't.

Oddly, I respected him.

After riding to Chula Vista for tacos, we raced through the sparse traffic on the freeway. The sound of the exhaust, the speed, the laughter, and the friendly goofing around proved to be too much. With each passing mile, I was slowly melting into a puddle of lust.

We excited the highway, and rolled to a stop at the traffic light.

"We're headed home, brother," Cholo shouted over the sound of his exhaust. "Lex is exhausted."

"Right on," Smoke said. "Your turn is one block up, right?"

Cholo checked the light and gave a nod.

Smoke revved his exhaust. "On green."

Cholo shook his head. "Damn it, Smoke."

Lex looked at me and grinned. "They do this all the time."

"No guts, no glory, motherfucker," Smoke taunted.

Cholo checked the light and then glanced at Smoke. "On green, asshole."

Lex clutched Cholo's waist like her life depended on it.

"Hold on," Smoke said over his shoulder. "Tight."

I wrapped my arms around his waist and sank my thumbs between the inside of his jeans and his hips. "Okay."

I watched as the cross-traffic light turned to yellow, and held my breath. The sound of the exhaust bellowed behind us in a deafening tone. When the light flashed from red to green, Smoke released the clutch.

We launched forward like we'd been rear-ended by a truck.

The back tire screeched, the front tire raised up, and we shot ahead of Cholo's bike by a few feet. Smoke leaned forward, pressing his chest onto the gas tank, and I followed, flattening my boobs against his back.

The exhilaration was something I hadn't ever felt.

He shifted gears, and Cholo caught up to us. After shifting again, Cholo passed us by a few feet. I took a quick look over Smoke's shoulder, and noticed we were going over 100 miles an hour.

My heart shot to my throat.

I glanced up. The light ahead turned to red. Both motorcycles, as if pre-programmed, decelerated, braked, and eventually came to a stop.

Smoke cocked his head to the side. "Lucky prick."

"Fuck you, Smoke." Cholo said. "My shit's faster. I outweigh you by thirty at least, and we're riding two up. That old sled is junk."

Smoke glared at him. "Two up?"

Cholo grinned. "Yeah. Me, Lex, and the baby."

The light changed to green.

"See ya, fat ass," Smoke shouted.

Lex waved, and they turned to the left. Without speaking, Smoke and I rode for a few miles through town. I enjoyed the relaxing ride just as much as the racing, but in a different way. For me, the motorcycle provided three things.

It was a mode of transportation, something very exciting, and it could also be very relaxing.

During our ride, I got lost in the smell of the ocean breeze, the low drone of the exhaust, and the feeling of having my arms wrapped around his waist. And then, he pulled into my driveway.

My heart sank.

I'd told myself this would be the last time we'd see each other, and after having such a wonderful night, I knew I'd have to honor my personal promise.

I thought of never seeing him again sickened me, but it was necessary.

He switched off the engine.

I removed my helmet, clutched it in my hands, and then took a slow deliberate breath.

One last time, that's it.

He stepped off the bike and reached for my hand. "Sorry about that race, but I just had to."

With the help of his guiding hand, I carefully got off the motorcycle. "Oh, that's okay. It was exciting."

He smiled, revealing dimples that I didn't know existed. "Glad you enjoyed it."

He took the helmet, put it in the compartment, and looked at me. His mouth twisted to one side, and he wagged his finger at me. "You remind me of that chick that sings country and dances on T.V."

I wondered who he was talking about, but his explanation didn't narrow my mental search to much less than 10,000 women.

"Oh yeah, *her*," I said sarcastically.

"*Burlesque*." He snapped his fingers, and then pointed at me. "She was in that, too. Won dancing with the stars a couple times."

I thought about it, and when it came to me, my eyes went wide. I swallowed hard, and stared at him in disbelief. "Julianne Hough?"

"Yeah," he said excitedly. "You look just like her. It's been buggin' me. Glad I figured it out."

I didn't want street races, fish tacos, and panty-melting compliments. I wanted him to be an asshole. I wanted him to fuck me one last time and leave angry after I said something sarcastic, pointed, and shitty.

I wanted him to not answer the late night drunken texts that I was sure would follow. I wanted him to eventually get so aggravated with me that he blocked my phone number. I wanted to tell him to get on his motorcycle and ride away. I wanted him to be angry and disappointed with me.

At least if he was it would make everything easier.

Instead, I reached for his hand. "Let's go in."

As soon as I extended my arm, I realized what I'd done. I expected him to pull away. In fact, I wanted him to. Filled completely with his compliment, I became lost in that moment. I'd simply forgotten who he was.

The unavailable single hot dad who just so happened to be a sexy biker.

His handsome looks made it easy to forget. In looking at his face, it was almost impossible to see him as anything other than gorgeous.

But, he didn't pull away.

He simply stepped beside me and followed me up the walk.

And, with each step we took, I lost a little more of my desire to push him away.

***

If it was going to be the last time, I decided it was going to be my way, or no way at all. He had no idea it was our final night together, and I had no idea of telling him. At least not yet.

I'd walked into the kitchen to get a bottle of water while he draped his kutte over the back of the couch. When I turned around, he was standing between me and the living room, wearing only his jeans and a wife beater.

The jeans were tight enough that they revealed a slight bulge in his crotch. Naturally, my eyes fell to it. The outline of his cock garnered my complete attention. After a moment of admiring his thickness, I took in each muscular inch of his long torso.

Upon reaching his eyes, I stopped.

I swallowed heavily, blindly reached for the counter, and parted my dry lips. "Come here."

With meaningful steps, he sauntered toward me. In those six strides, his swagger seduced me. Denying his bravado was impossible. When he walked, it was a firm reminder of the sexual beast that dwelled in his being.

"I want your cock." I said, the words barely escaping my lips audibly.

Without responding, he reached for his belt. With my eyes fixed on his tattooed hand, I watched as he lowered his jeans past his hips. As his thick shaft sprung free, my throat went tight.

RIGID

I dropped the water bottle.

His jeans and the bottle hit the floor at the same time.

With my eyes glued to his twitching cock, I fumbled to rid myself of my shorts and panties. Like a high school teen in her first sexual encounter, I struggled with the denim fabric for an inordinate amount of time.

"Here," he said.

I watched intently as he pulled my shorts down my thighs, taking my panties with them in the process. With care, he lifted each of my feet, pulled the shorts free, and then cast them aside.

"Thanks," I said, but the words were silent.

He didn't bother standing.

Kneeling at my feet, he stared at my pussy for a few seconds, and then looked up.

I swallowed hard.

His mouth twisted into a smirk.

He buried his face between my legs, took my wet mound into his mouth, and then flicked his tongue against my clit. Again, and again, the tip of his tongue tickled my swollen nub.

A tingling ran through me and my legs went weak. I reached for the counter, found it, and then sucked in a breath. With my head tilted back and my eyes pinched closed, I stood on shaking legs and tried to focus on what he was doing to me.

When he touched me, the feelings he created were new. Convinced he was a master at the art of sex, and that I was his student, I eagerly allowed him to continue, excited to experience whatever it was he was introducing me to.

The licking stopped. My eyes opened, and I looked down.

He glanced up. "Your pussy tastes like honey."

I couldn't speak. I simply bit into my bottom lip and nodded.

And, once again, he buried his face between my thighs.

I gulped a breath as he pushed a finger deep inside me. He added another, and I twisted my hips back and forth in response.

While his fingers fucked me slowly and predictably, he began to suck my clit.

Don't stop.

Please, God.

Don't. Let. Him. Stop.

With my clit pinched between his soft lips, he began to moan. A buzzing ran through me from his mouth to nipples. Pressure built within me. I arched my back, opened my mouth, and cried out, but it escaped me as a silent gasp.

My eyes shot open and then fell to the floor.

In my kitchen, I had the baddest of badass bikers on his knees – sucking my pussy like a boss. For that instant, my life was a dream.

I gripped his head firmly in my hands and commenced to fuck his mouth, hoping he wouldn't object.

His moaning continued, growing more prominent with each thrust of my hips.

My knees buckled.

I struggled to remain standing, forcing my pussy hard against his mouth in the process. In return, his fingers pushed deeper.

My muscles tensed, and then relaxed. Every ounce of emotion that had slowly built within me exploded.

His fingers continued, in and out of my wetness. His tongue teased my clit. His free hand gripped my ass, pulling me into him firmly.

The orgasms continued, one after the other, until my legs collapsed.

He caught me before I hit the floor, and lifted me into his arms. While he carried me into the bedroom, I studied his face.

I wished, with each step that he took, that things could be different between us.

But, they couldn't, and I knew it.

Knowing it saddened me.

As he laid me on the bed, I decided to live in that moment, and that moment only, realizing it would be our last night together. It had to be. I couldn't continue without falling in love with him, that I was sure of.

He tossed his shirt aside while I recovered from my trip to sexual outer space, and then he rolled to the side and looked at me. He'd already seduced me with his walk, and now he was doing so with his eyes.

"I want to ride your cock," I whispered.

His mouth curled into a guilty smile, and he gripped his cock in his fist. "Come get it."

My pussy was dripping wet. I straddled him, and then watched as he guided the tip of his swollen cock between my legs. As it disappeared into my wetness, one thick inch at a time, my breath escaped me and my eyes went closed.

Once he was inside me fully, I opened my eyes and gazed into his.

He was perfect.

But he was unavailable and incapable of becoming attached.

This is it.

One last time.

I wrapped my hands firmly around his calves, arched my back, and then rode his stiff cock like I was trying out for the sexual Olympics.

When it was over, and he was long gone, I wanted him to realize just what he was missing. I hoped to convince him that I was different, and the only way I knew to do so was by fucking him like he'd never been fucked before.

I wanted him to want me no differently than I wanted him.

I released his legs, and dug my fingers into his thick chest. His eyes went wide as I sank my fingernails into his flesh, bucking my hips wildly the entire time, milking his thick cock with each complete stroke.

"Fuck, you feel good," he moaned.

"You like my tight pussy?"

He squeezed my tits firmly in his hands. "Fuck yes."

"I. Love. Your. Fucking. Cock." I said, barking out one word with each thrust of my hips.

He gazed directly into my eyes, and then grinned. "I. Can. Fucking. Tell."

I allowed myself to become immersed in his eyes, which for some reason seemed to have turned from blue to grey. With his gaze fixed on mine, I writhed and bucked my hips, hoping to find that perfect position.

The one that would send me to the moon.

I rolled my shoulders, arched my back, and ground against the length of his thick shaft.

Oh fuck.

The tip of his dick rubbed against my g-spot. I closed my eyes and exhaled heavily. While I got lost in the feeling of his cock against the most sensual spot I possessed, his hands kneaded my boobs with perfection.

Firm enough that I knew who was in control, but not so harsh that it was uncomfortable, he squeezed my tits masterfully. Every few seconds, he'd pinch my nipples between his thumb and forefinger, and when he did, a tingling sensation ran from my boobs to the tip of his perfect cock.

I lifted my hands, arched my back further, and reached for his ankles.

Oh my fucking fuck.

Fuck yes.

Don't. Fucking. Move.

My eyes rolled back so far it hurt. My lips parted slightly. "Don't. Change. Anything. Don't move."

With my legs spread so wide I ached, I forced my ass against his thighs. The smooth skin of the head of his cock continued to torture me, grinding against my g-spot. I moved my hips ever so slightly, sending an electric shock through me with each movement.

I bit against my lip and closed my eyes.

I felt myself reaching climax.

Like a volcano preparing to erupt, the pressure built within me until it could build no more. And then, at that instant when the act of fucking goes from physical to spiritual, his cock swelled.

My pussy contracted, clenching it like a vise.

His breathing became labored.

"I'm going to…"

"So am I," he breathed.

Together, magically, we reached the brink.

I felt as if I burst into a million sensual pieces, showering the room with emotion. I wanted to cry, scream, dig my nails into his flesh, and die, all at the same time.

Instead, I opened my mouth and said nothing.

Because I wasn't able.

I was frozen in time. It only lasted a nanosecond, but I was frozen nevertheless.

Almost as if I was hovering over him, looking down upon his climactic finish, I watched as he erupted inside of me.

His jaw stretched wide, and he let out a growl with the intensity of a powerful beast. His eyes met mine, and he smiled a shallow and slightly guilty grin.

As countless micro-orgasms shot through me, I collapsed onto his chest, incapable of holding myself up for one more second. I remained motionless for some time, and then raised my head from his shoulder and looked him in the eyes.

I knew he enjoyed it just as much as I did, but he'd never admit it, and that saddened me. I wanted to hold him, hug him, and tell him how good it felt to fuck him, but I didn't dare.

I wasn't some sappy weirdo who was falling in love after fucking him twice. In fact, I was far from it. But I liked him. I liked looking at him. I liked fucking him. And, I loved how his cock made me feel. I wanted to get to know him, and in doing so, allow him to get to know me.

I wanted to do all the things he wanted me to do, each one without instruction. I wanted to know his deepest of desires, and hoped I could satisfy each one of them.

Yet.

The way it felt knowing all we would ever have was sex crushed those wants and desires into dust.

For whatever reason, admitting I was nothing but a hole for him to fill hurt me. And, I'd been hurt too many times in the past to allow it to happen again.

I rolled to the side, stood, and turned toward the bathroom. Facing away from him, I cleared my throat. "Do you…uhhm. Do you mind…

would you just let yourself out?"

God.

This hurts.

"Wow. Really?"

I didn't bother turning around. I couldn't allow him to see my face. Hiding my feelings at that moment would have been impossible, and if he knew how I truly felt, any rejection that followed would surely crush me.

"I'm going to shower," I said. "I'll take my time. I'd appreciate it if you'd be gone when I came out."

He cleared his throat. "Alright."

While I showered, I came close to crying several times. It seemed ridiculous for me to feel the way I felt, but Smokey was different.

I could sense it.

I could feel it.

And, I could see it.

But. His unique situation wouldn't allow him to accept anyone in his life that caused him to *feel*.

I dried off, got dressed, and walked into the kitchen. Although the home was void of his presence, his scent still lingered in the air. I closed my eyes, inhaled a shallow breath, and shuddered at the smell of him.

I opened my eyes.

A folded piece of paper laying on the countertop caught my eye. I walked toward it. On the outside of the note, my name was written.

I eagerly unfolded it.

The script was handwritten, and elegant.

Sandy,

You satisfied me more in two days than you'll ever know. If you're thinking this comment is about sex, you're wrong.

It's about your fun-loving attitude, your great personality, and the way you put up with my shit.

For a minute, you tricked me into thinking I was normal.

But, I'm not.

Probably be best if we called it quits.

I'm enjoying this too much.

Smokey

I read the note, and then re-read it.

With reluctance, I folded the note, walked to the trash can, and dropped it inside.

SIX

Smokey

It had been a week since I'd seen Sandy last, and Cholo and I were a foreclosure property that he'd purchased to flip for a profit. I'd expressed my disappointment in knowing I would never see her again, and Cholo seemed shocked by the decision.

While I took the last of my measurements, he loomed over me with his hands on his hips.

"You're a fucking weirdo," he said.

I extended the end of the tape measure to the wall, made note of the dimension, and wrote it down.

"Says who?" I asked over my shoulder.

"Says me."

"If I valued your opinion, I might give a shit about that remark. But I don't, so I don't."

"You ever think that having a woman around your daughter might help matters?"

Cholo wasn't the Filthy Fuckers Sergeant-at-Arms, but he was the club's enforcer. A bald-headed former boxer who was built like a body builder, he wasn't a man to get sideways with.

Regardless, his comment hit a nerve, and I was ready to fight him, if need be.

RIGID

I stood, clipped the tape measure to my pocket, and shot him a laser sharp glare. "And what in the absolute fuck makes you think matters around my house need help?"

"I'm just saying--"

"And, I'm just saying that you better back the fuck up, or you and I are gonna tussle, motherfucker. Don't fuck with my daughter. She ain't the club's business, and friend or not, she sure as fuck ain't any of yours."

He tugged against the bill of his cap and shot me a look. "God damn, Smoke. You said you liked that Sandy chick, but that you weren't going to see her any more. Lex says she's a damned good chick. I was just trying to say…" He clenched his jaw and shook his head. "Fuck it. I said what I had to say. No disrespect intended."

I gave a nod. "None taken. I'm short tempered right now. Sorry."

"Something you want to talk about?"

I knelt, took another measurement, and then wrote it down. "Daughter turns seventeen in three weeks."

"Is that a big deal?"

"Around my house, it is."

"Why's that?"

"She starts dating when she's seventeen."

"Kind of a late start, huh?"

I looked at him, cocked my eyebrow, and gave him one of Eddie's famous stink eyes.

He raised his hands in the air and turned his palms toward me. "Sounds like the perfect age to start dating to me."

I glanced at the sheet of paper, did the math, and looked up. "Fifteen grand even. Don't fuck with me about it, Cholo. That tile that's got to come up in the back bathroom is asbestos, and there ain't another flooring contractor that'll do this job for a penny under eighteen. Make a counter offer, and you can find another tile man."

"Fifteen's fine," he said with a nod.

I stood, picked up my notepad, and wiped the dust from my jeans. "Sixteen is too fucking young, if you ask me. And, making her wait until she's eighteen's is cruel. So, at my house, seventeen's the age for dating. She told me the other night I was a sadist."

"Your daughter did?"

I nodded. "Yep. Said preventing her from going on dates was whittling away at the fiber of her being, and the end result was that I'd pummeled her confidence into a pile of mush. She compared what was left of it to a bowl of grits."

His brow wrinkled. "What the fuck are grits?"

"Boiled ground corn. Or hominy. Nasty shit, if you ask me. It's a southern thing."

"Like oatmeal?"

I shrugged. "Cream of Wheat."

"You smashed her self-esteem into Cream of Wheat, huh?"

"She said I pummeled it. Same difference, I suppose."

"Was she serious?"

"Nope. She's like me, if you can imagine that. She's dramatic, full of shit, and rarely cracks a smile. People that don't know her think she's serious, but she's laughing at 'em on the inside."

"Sounds like you."

"She's a good kid. But in three weeks I'm gonna start interviewing her potential dates, and it scares the shit out of me. I'll have my pistol in my lap when I talk to 'em, though."

"I don't envy you, that's for sure."

"Find out what you and Lex are having yet?"

"Nope. Can't for a while. Too early, the doc said. I think it's a girl, though."

I nodded. "Girls are cool. Easy to get attached to 'em if you ask me."

"A boy would be cool, too." After gazing down at the discolored tile for a moment, he looked up. "You saying you wouldn't love a boy the same way?"

"The way I said that sounded bad, huh?"

He chuckled, tugged against the bill of his cap, and looked at me. "Yeah."

"You love Lex, right?"

"Fuck yeah."

"Can you think of anyone that could replace her? Like, step into your life, take her place, and satisfy you as much?"

"That's a stupid fucking question," he snapped back. "Fuck no."

"Well, you can take that love and multiply it times a thousand, and that'd be a fucking molecule of the love you feel for your kid. Just wait, you'll see. Boy or girl don't matter, you'll love 'em, and you'll get attached to 'em, too."

He lifted the bill of his cap. "What you're saying doesn't make sense, Brother."

"Girls need sheltered from fuckers like us. Protected, or whatever. Providing that protection draws us closer to 'em, but it's different than love. It's hard to explain. A parent ends up thriving for that provision. To be the one who they turn to when they need something, or when they're in pain. Girls always need someone to go to. Someone they can count on."

"Makes sense," he said. "Kind of."

"We act out of love naturally, but I think it's the interaction that we become attached to. The conversations we have, and seeing their growth. Bottles to baby food. Crawling to walking. Talking. Learning how to read. Middle school to high school. Oh, and diapers to potty training." I chuckled. "Wait till your kids drops a fuckin' log in the hallway and doesn't tell you, and then you step on it. I about broke my fuckin' neck one night on one of Eddie's random turds."

"Not looking forward to that."

"You say that now, but just wait. A day will come when you'll wish like hell you had a shitty diaper to change. And, not having it'll make you sick."

For me, that day had long since passed.

And, I wished like hell it hadn't.

SEVEN

Sandy

Dancing was a job. Some looked at it as more; a stepping stone or gateway to being an actress. I knew better. The club was a place for the dreamers to gather. The dancers who dreamt of something better than what they had at home, and the patrons who dreamt of the same.

I looked at dancing differently than most people, and while doing so, compared myself to an actress. When I was on stage, I was playing a part. The people who came to watch me were no different than those who flocked to see the latest installment of the Fifty Shades movies.

I opened the car door, got one foot out the door, and doubled over in pain. Drowning my sorrows in an all-you-can-eat Thai buffet wasn't a terrible idea, but the hole in the wall I chose to do it at wasn't one of the best decisions I'd ever made. When the pain diminished, I stepped out of the car and ran toward the back door.

I knocked on the door three times, paused, and then knocked once.

Craig pulled the door open, saw me, and smiled. "Out of breath, as always."

I pressed my hands to my knees, gulped a breath, and grinned. "Hey."

"How's it going?"

I wedged myself between his massive thigh and the door frame. "Not good. I ate Thai food at *Thai-cos* last night."

He stepped to the side and wrinkled his nose. "The place that sells tacos on one side and Chinese food on the other?"

"It's Thai, not Chinese. Thai-cos, get it?"

He shrugged. "I don't partake."

"It won't happen again. I've been sick all day."

Craig was one of the bouncers, and was also a close friend. He was tall, muscular, and looked like a professional wrestler. His head was shaved, he wore a neatly-trimmed goatee, and his skin was as smooth as glass. As with all the bouncers, he was gay, which was one of the owner's prerequisites for male employees at the bar.

According to the owner, it eliminated the drama between the dancers and the male staff members. The owners only other rule, *no boyfriends allowed in the club*, was strictly enforced. This left the club drama reduced to the arguments with the dancers.

But it was enough drama to satisfy even the most dramatic of the drama queens.

"Starla didn't make it," Craig said. "And Neveah's still sick. So, we're short staffed tonight. Might need you to stay 'till close."

I'd been exhausted for the last few days, more than likely the result of slight depression. Nothing would help me get my mind off Smoke more than working until I was exhausted even more.

"That's fine," I said. "I can use the money."

He glanced at his watch. "I rotate to the stage in a few, so I'll be on the floor when you're up."

I shouldered my bag and peered toward the dressing room. "Good. I'll see you in a few."

If there was a drama free zone in a strip club, the dressing room wasn't it. Boyfriend problems, girlfriend problems, baby daddy problems, missing tip money, babysitter problems, and lap dances gone bad were some of the typical concerns. The discussions were never simple, and always seemed to either turn into an argument or a fight.

After three years, it was getting old.

Sitting at the vanity preparing for her shift, Nikki glanced over her right shoulder. "Hey, Texxxas."

I smiled. "Hey."

Diamond turned to face me and widened her eyes comically. "Guess what George did? After you left last night?"

I tossed my bag on the vanity. "Uhhm. I don't know, what?"

She cocked her hip, shot Nikki a shitty glare, and then looked at me. "Tipped me $500, and then asked me out."

"Any guy will ask you out if you jack him off in a booth," Nikki said without turning around.

Nikki was one to talk, she gave her regulars blowjobs when she could get away with it. I looked at her and then at Diamond's reflection in the mirror. "Are you going to go out with him?"

"Yeah." She gave Nikki another glare, and then looked at me. "Do you know what he drives?"

I had no idea, and I really didn't care. I did my best to feign interest and shrugged. "Uhhm. No. What?"

"Mercedes."

"A twenty-year old Mercedes," Nikki chimed.

"She's jealous," Diamond said. "Can you tell?"

Nikki spun around. "I doubt he tipped you more than $10. Form what I hear, your hand jobs suck. And, jealous of what?"

"Jealous of the $500 tip, and because he asked me out. What do you get? $20 for a blowy, right?"

Nikki turned around. A strip of eyelashes dangled from the tip of her finger. "No, I get a grand, a ride in a *new* Mercedes, and a lobster dinner."

Diamond picked up her sweats, waved her free hand toward Nikki, and rolled her eyes. "Jealous bitch."

"A fifty-year-old surfer let you give him a handy, and then asked you out while you were wiping the cum off his disgusting gut. What is there to be jealous of?"

"He's not fifty. And he owns a construction company."

Nikki leaned forward, pressed the eyelashes in place, and then fanned her face with her hands. "He's probably a janitor, and he looks fifty."

Diamond cocked her hip. "He's not fifty. He's got a teenage dick, *and* a Mercedes."

"Give it a rest, *Theresa*."

"Don't call me that," Diamond hissed.

Nikki picked up another strip of eyelashes and then glanced over her shoulder. "It's your name."

"We're not supposed to use our names, and you know it. Mark will have your ass, you spiteful bitch."

My stomach knotted, and I bent over in response.

"Are you okay, Tex?" Nikki asked.

After a few seconds, the pain went away. I looked at her and shook my head. "Bad Thai food."

"Nothing's worse," she said. "Where?"

"Thai-cos."

"Oh my God. Why?"

"All you can eat. I was in a mood."

"A mood for food poisoning." She nodded her head toward my waist.

"You'll pay for it."

Diamond pulled on her sweats, slipped her arms through her hoodie, and then zipped it up. "I guess I'm out of here."

"Only reason you stuck around was to brag to Texxxas," Nikki said. "Go."

She grabbed her purse, shot Nikki a look, and then turned toward the door. "Bye Texxxas."

I waved. "See ya, Diamond."

Nikki leaned forward, checked her makeup, and then looked at me. She batted her lashes a few times.

"They look good, as always," I said.

She smiled. "You're so sweet."

"You always look good." I said. It was true, she looked great, she just didn't look her age. She was 21 years old, and looked like she was 35. A really hot 35-year-old, but 35, nonetheless.

She shook her head lightly, and then looked in the mirror. "You come in here, put on your outfit, and walk on stage. No one else here can think about doing that. We've got to work for it."

"I'm just a take me or leave me kind of girl," I said. "That's how we are in Texas."

I wasn't really from Texas, but none of the girls knew it. I was from New Mexico. The daughter of an alcoholic mother who had a second job as a drug addict, and a father who decided he'd had enough of her when I was six, I left when I was thirteen and went to live with my aunt and uncle.

When I was seventeen, I graduated high school. I thanked them for their hospitality, loaded my belongings into my Volkswagen, and left. Hoping to land a job as an actress, I made my way to Southern

California. Upon arriving, I realized I was no different than the other 40 million people who lived there. Disappointed, but not defeated, I got a job as a waitress, saved my money, and bought a set of boobs.

"Well, I'm from the SD," she said. "It's competitive in SoCal."

I laughed at the thought of her and Diamond arguing about the $500 hand job. "It sure is."

As I was changing, I noticed a little spotting on my panties. After cleaning up and getting my outfit on, I turned toward Nikki. "It's the 22nd, right?"

"21st. Why?"

I shook my head. "Just wondering."

She looked me over. "That outfit is on point. Can't go wrong with a school girl get up, that's for sure."

"We'll see," I said.

I looked at my reflection in the mirror. I was dressed like Britney Spears in the *Hit Me Baby One More Time* Video. I cleared my head of thoughts of Smokey. Then, I prayed to see right through whoever happened to be on sniffers row.

The music stopped, and then I heard the DJ dismiss Rose.

I took a deep breath and waited.

"Here's what you've been waiting all night for. Gentlemen, the one and only. Standing five foot seven, and only 114 pounds, she's got a set of natural double D's that are the envy of the industry. Give it up, motherfuckers. This. Is. Texxxas!"

As Buckcherry's *Crazy Bitch* began to blare over the sound system, Texxxas walked out onto the stage no differently than a Victoria's Secret model walks up the runway.

When she did, she left Sandy in the dressing room.

Where she was safe from everyone and everything that Texxxas didn't have the common sense to fear.

The men shouted and cheered. Money rained onto the stage. And, she danced like it was the last time she'd ever have the chance.

EIGHT

Smokey

I rolled past the gate, across the narrow strip of asphalt, and through the open doors of the shop. As my bike came to a stop beside Pee Bee's bagger, I whacked the throttle twice. After making sure Crip was pissed off, I shut down the engine, pulled off my helmet, and stepped over the seat.

"How many fucking times have I told you not to rev that piece of shit up in the shop? Motherfuckers in Los Angeles can hear that loud son-of-a-bitch," Crip complained.

Crip was the president of the club, a former Navy SEAL, and a pain in my respective ass. He wasn't arrogant, but he was damned fucking close. His *don't rev your engine in the shop* rule was one of the many rules he had that I didn't like, or respect.

Bikers revved their engines.

Especially in confined spaces.

I pulled my vape from my pocket, took a long pull, and exhaled it in his direction. "My bad, Brother. Shit, I forgot."

"You always fucking forget."

I shrugged. "I can't remember shit."

He glared at me, and then folded his arms across his chest.

I considered folding my arms in a similar fashion just to piss him off,

73

but realized if I did, I wouldn't be able to blow smoke in his face. So, I decided not to.

The club's Sergeant-at-Arms, Pee Bee, was leaning against the workbench with a bottle of beer dangling from his fingertips. Standing 6'-8" and solid muscle from head to toe, he was an intimidating motherfucker, but his heart was made of gold.

I glared at Crip until he broke my gaze, and then gave Pee Bee a nod.

"What's shakin', motherfucker?" he asked.

"Just trying to make enough money to buy a new set of cams," I said. "Cholo whipped my ass the other night, and I'm sick of it. How's things?"

He shrugged. "Things are good."

I looked at Crip. "So, what's the emergency, Crip?"

"No emergency. Just need to figure something out." He glanced at my vape and then shook his head. "Ought to make a rule against those motherfuckers in the shop."

I raised my vape. "Against this?"

He nodded.

I pressed the *fire* button, inhaled for as long as I could, and exhaled a flume of vapor so large that it encompassed them both. "Let me know when you do, I'll turn in my kutte."

He waved his hands, frantically trying to clear the air in front of him. "That shit's going to end up killing us."

I folded my arms over my chest and shot him a glare. "And you pricks getting drunk and riding in the front of formation will end up killing the entire club."

"That's different," he said. "I'm serious."

"*I'm* serious. Make a one-beer limit. Then, add something against farting and fucking to the bylaws. And loud noises. Oh, and leaving oil spots on your precious fucking concrete floor. Make a rule against scratching our nuts, too. Outsiders might see it as pretentious. They'd see us as the big cocked biker club. Hell, that'd be the end of us."

He crossed his arms, looked me up and down, and then met my gaze. "I'm about sick and fucking tired of that attitude, Smoke."

Shielded from Crip's view, Pee Bee cocked and eyebrow and grinned. He knew the remark would irritate me, and was obviously waiting eagerly for my response.

"I'm about sick and fucking tired of you being an arrogant prick," I said.

He flexed his biceps. "Come again?"

"You heard me." I lifted my chin slightly and waited for his blood to boil.

His face went flush. He inhaled a shallow breath and jutted his chest out. I coughed out a laugh and nodded toward the SEAL tattoo on his upper arm. "What am I supposed to do now? Lower my head and tell you I'm sorry?"

He took another short breath, and I was sure a response was coming, but I didn't give him a chance to speak. I waved my hand toward Pee Bee. "Peeb here can't do wrong in your eyes, and Cholo's pretty close to the same. Rowdy could come burn this shop down, and you'd help him clean up the fucking mess. Me? I smoke my vape and rev my motor, and you're ready to crucify me. You treat P-Nut the same fucking way. Always on his ass. Consistency, motherfucker. I want consistency. Equality--"

His hands shot to his hips. "You fucking done?"

I shook my head. "Did I sound like I was done? You fucking

interrupted me. That's what I'm talking about. Give and get, asshole. Give respect. You'll get it back."

"Jesus, Smokey. I treat you with respect. I treat all the fellas with respect. You're a prick most of the time, and I act accordingly."

I shrugged. "And you're a prick *all the time*, and *I* act accordingly."

He exhaled heavily, and then shook his head. "You're tough to take, Smoke. You pissed?"

I took a pull on my vape, and then grinned. "Nope."

"Irritated?"

I tilted my head back, blew the smoke toward the ceiling, and then looked him in the eyes. "Nope."

"You think I'm a prick?"

"Nope." I grinned. "I *know* you're a prick."

"God damn it," he snapped back.

"But I can live with it," I said. "I signed on for this shit, and you were a prick on that day, so I knew what I was getting into. What's up? Why the meeting?"

"Peeb's here because Peeb's always here. I wanted to talk to you about Tank."

"The prospect? The Marine?"

"Yep."

"Don't know the kid. What about him?"

"Meathead got locked up over the weekend for a firearms charge. He was in LA over the weekend, got in a fight in a bar, and pulled a pistol on some prick in the parking lot. Someone called the cops, and must have given a pretty good description, because the feds picked him up this morning on a firearms violation. There's no bond set, and it sounds like they're going to railroad his ass. He'll do a dime if he does a day."

I wasn't sure how Meat being in jail affected me, and as much as I didn't want to hear Crip's explanation, I felt compelled to ask anyway. "Sucks about Meat, he was good people. How do I fit into this, though?"

"Wantin' you to take his prospect."

I spit out a laugh. "Shit there for a second I thought you said you wanted me to take that prospect to raise."

He didn't so much as crack a smile. He simply raised his eyebrows and waited.

"I've got one kid, Crip." I shook my head and chuckled another laugh. "Don't need another."

"I'm serious, Smoke. I need you to take this kid. Show him the ropes. He's a good kid. He'll make a good patch."

"I ain't even been here two years. And, I didn't vouch for that prick, Meat did. Peeb's been here for what? Ten years? Give him to Peeb."

"You'll make a better mentor," he said. "You never ride drunk, you don't take any shit, and you're not afraid to stand your ground. You've got a sixth sense when it comes to threats, and that's not something anyone else in this club has. Short of me, that is. You're rigid in your beliefs, Smokey. And, as much as you might disagree, I respect you for it."

"As a biker, in his beliefs, or in bed, there's only one way for a man to be," I said dryly. "Rigid."

Crip gave a nod.

I looked at Pee Bee.

He raised his bottle of beer and gave me his signature smirk. "It's only eight months."

"Eight fucking months." My eyes fell to the floor. "Jesus."

"It'll pass quick."

77

I shifted my eyes to Crip. "What if I say no?"

"I'll be disappointed. Kid might not make it. Then again, he might make it, and end up being a turd because Fat Larry or Buck takes him."

"Give him to P-Nut."

He shook his head. "P-Nut's inconsistent, and he's nuttier than a fuckin' fruitcake."

He was right about the Nut, but the last thing I wanted to do was mentor a war-torn Marine who was seeking a place to expel his aggression. "God damn it, Crip. I'd rather not. Kid's probably got PTSD. If he flips out on me, I'll put hands on his ass."

"I'm sure he *does* have PTSD. Get to know him." He shrugged. "Part of being a mentor. Talk to him. Find out who he is. Show him the ropes."

"I've got plenty of other shit to--"

He nodded toward my bike. "Have him put cams in your bike. Have him help you with tile work. Use him up."

I was an asshole, there was no denying it. I'd been one my entire adult life, and for good reason. If people's perception of me was that I was a complete prick, they didn't attach themselves to me emotionally. And, if we left feelings at the door, I didn't have to worry about being hurt by another rotten cold-hearted bitch.

Truth be known, deep down inside, I wasn't a prick. It was a façade. A mask. Something I wore to protect me from the throngs of people I was sure were destined to cause me harm.

I looked at my bike, and then at Crip. Ultimately, I wanted what was best for the club. I was sure there wasn't a snowball's chance in hell that this kid was going to do anything to hurt me. He might be a pain in the ass for eight months, but I could stand anything for eight months.

"Fine, I'll mentor the little prick."

Crip slapped his hand against my bicep and then made a fist. "Appreciate ya, Smoke."

I pounded my fist into his. "Just want what's best for the club."

The next eight months were going to be hell for at least one of us, that was for sure.

NINE

Sandy

I sat up, looked around the bedroom, and then glanced at the clock. I normally didn't wake up at 6:30 in the morning, especially after closing at the club. My growling stomach gave a hint as to why I woke up early, and although I considered going back to sleep, the continued protest from my digestive system won the argument.

I rolled out of bed, walked to the kitchen, and made some toast. I tried to remember the last time I'd eaten, and realized the Thai food I'd eaten thirty-six hours earlier was my last meal. I devoured the first piece, making a cup of espresso as I ate. After drinking half the coffee, I bit into the second piece of toast and paused.

Oh shit.

I ran to the bathroom and slid to a stop with my arms wrapped around the toilet. Five minutes later, my toast and the morning's caffeine were in the toilet, and I was back at square one.

What in the Thai-co fuck?

I washed my face, looked in the mirror, and wondered just what happened when I took the Mex-Asian buffet adventure. Certain I was battling a bad case of food poisoning, I walked to the bedroom, got my phone, and asked my all-knowing friend, *Google*.

I typed in my question, *how long does food poisoning last,* pressed the *search* button and waited for the page to load. In a few seconds, I was astounded at the results. I could expect to be sick for between 2 and 10 days.

Jesus.

Aggravated at Google's response, and hoping it might be something else, I typed in, *what causes nausea after eating breakfast*, and pressed *search*.

I opened the first page, and then read the potential causes in order.

Food allergies.

I knew I wasn't allergic to toast or coffee, so I scrolled to the next one.

Food poisoning

I already knew the possibilities of food poisoning, the symptoms, and the recovery time, so I scrolled past it and to the next.

Stomach virus

I decided it was quite possible that I had the flu, but the symptoms were more erratic, and inconsistent than any flu I'd previously experienced. Certain it wasn't the flu, I thumbed the page up.

Pregnancy

I laughed. Then, I stared at the phone. In a moment, my stomach sank. My mind raced, arguing with itself about the possibility. I was on the pill, and Smokey had a vasectomy, so it wasn't even possible, but for whatever reason, I couldn't convince myself otherwise.

I Googled *morning sickness symptoms*, then stared blankly at the results.

- Persistent excessive vomiting (more than 3 or 4 times a day)
- Unrelenting, severe nausea.

- ☐ Dehydration.
- ☐ A decrease in urination due to dehydration.
- ☐ Maternal weight loss or failure to gain weight.
- ☐ Rapid heartbeat.
- ☐ Headaches and confusion.

Short of the rapid heartbeat, I was experiencing them all. Frantic, I searched *early symptoms of pregnancy*. The results weren't what I was hoping for.

Food aversions. Mood swings. Frequent urination Fatigue. Sore breasts. Light bleeding. Spotting. Nausea.

I swallowed heavily, then re-read them.

It was impossible, and it wasn't what I wanted. Not at all. The situation, if it was in fact the situation, couldn't be worse.

Furthermore, being pregnant with Smokey's baby would ruin my life's dreams, completely. I wanted to fall in love, get engaged, marry, buy a home, and then have a baby. I'd saved almost every cent I'd made over the last three years, but it was nowhere near enough to raise a child.

Especially alone.

I tossed my phone on the couch, flopped my head in my hands, and began to cry. When the crying stopped, I came to my senses and realized although my little fairy tale didn't work out, my life still could.

All I needed to do was allow whatever was supposed to happen, happen.

God's will, not mine.

The first thing I needed to do was to take a pregnancy test.

Regardless of the outcome, I'd have to find a way to live with the results.

My uncle Ramon always used to say, *there's only one way to keep from getting pregnant. Abstinence.*

If I was willing to take the risk, I had to be willing to live with the results. I wiped my tears, stared at my phone, and prayed for God's will, not mine.

Then, I drove to the CVS.

***

Until I met Lex, I really didn't have any friends that were girls. I'd always found girls to be catty and spiteful, so my friends were limited to the bouncers at the bar, or the man I was *dating*. The men I dated was an ever-changing list, but there was one person I remained close to, regardless.

Craig gave me a hug, and then looked me over. He raised his hands to my face, swept his thumbs beneath my eyes, and did his best to clear the mascara from my cheeks. "There."

"Was it bad?"

The corner of his mouth curled up. "You looked like you were trying out for an M. Night Shyamalan movie."

"Who's that?"

"It doesn't...never mind. You look great now, and that's all that matters." He stepped to the side and waved his arm toward the living room. "Come in."

I slipped past him, and upon seeing his living room, stopped and stared. It looked totally different than the last time I had visited.

"Oh my God, this looks fantastic. Everything's new."

"I got bored."

An awesome display of retro contemporary furniture was neatly fitted into his small condo. I found the various shapes and colors exciting, and wished my apartment looked the same. I considered sitting on the white

SCOTT HILDRETH

leather sectional, and then opted for an orange fabric chair that had a wide seat cushion, high arms, and a very shallow back.

"That's great to look at, but it's terrible to sit in," he said.

I sat down, and immediately agreed. I pointed toward a turquoise leather chair across from the sectional. "What about that?"

He nodded. "It's fun."

I tossed my purse on the coffee table, sank into the turquoise chair, and looked around the room. "This is awesome."

"Thank you. Would you like something to drink?"

"Water?"

"You're so easy."

If you only knew.

He returned in a moment, and handed me a bottle of water and a glass. "What's going on? I know you didn't come over for a glass of water."

"I need an opinion."

He smiled and sat down on the sectional. "You came to the right place."

Dressed in black and gray spandex exercise pants and a dark gray Under Armour shirt, he reminded me of Dwayne Johnson. He even cocked his eyebrow the same manner, and I often wondered if he practiced in front of the mirror.

I took a drink from the bottle, and then poured the glass full. As I watched the bubbles come to the surface, I considered how I wanted to start the conversation.

I'd spent the last hour and a half feeling a wide range of emotions. Initially angry, my anger soon changed to fear. Then, I felt content. Happy. Somehow, I became satisfied that I could handle the situation.

85

Throughout it all, though, there was one constant.

I was alone.

I picked up the glass and gazed into it. "I've got myself into a situation."

"I'm sure we can figure it out. Want to enlighten me a little more?"

I nodded, but didn't immediately respond. I didn't know if I could. There was a big difference between silently accepting my pregnancy and speaking about it.

"I uhhm." I looked up, inhaled a deep breath, and then gave the news. "I'm. I'm pregnant."

He smiled and raised his glass. "Congratulations."

Of all the things he could have said, he said *that*. At first, I was shocked. Then, I was grateful. He knew I'd been out of a relationship for a few months, and I would have expected his reaction to be one of shock. His immediate acceptance was reassuring, but seemed out of place.

"Thanks," I said, my voice thick with sarcasm.

"You don't sound happy."

"Should I be?"

"I think so." He sat up straight and locked eyes with me. "Do you know how many people it takes to make a difference in this world?"

"Uhhm. I don't know. A lot. Why?"

"It takes *one*."

Our conversation had taken a left turn, and I wasn't prepared. I wanted to talk about my pregnancy, and it seemed he wanted to talk about something totally different. I lowered my glass and blinked a few times. "Huh?"

"William Shakespeare. Nelson Mandela. Charles Darwin. Albert

Einstein. As individuals, they each made a contribution that changed the course of history. God has given you an opportunity to raise a child. Someone that very well could be the next Martin Luther King. You should be grateful. It was his gift to you."

It was an interesting concept, but I had hoped for a less philosophical approach. I set my glass on the coffee table and let out a sigh. "I don't know what to do."

"Be responsible. Do the right thing."

I didn't want him to tell me what to do, I wanted him to tell me what *not* to do. "What would be the wrong thing?"

He shrugged. "Neglect?"

Once again, not what I was after. Frustrated, I shook my head and then looked right at him. "The father has a grown kid, and he doesn't do relationships. Well, she's kind of grown. She's seventeen."

He scrunched his nose. "He was absent in the child's *and* the mother's lives?"

"No. The mother left when the baby was born, and he raised the baby. She lives with him. But, she's not a baby. Not anymore, anyway."

"Single father?"

I nodded. "Yep."

"Has he always been single? Since the baby was born?"

"That's what he said."

"Is he nice looking? Does he have a good personality? Is he a good person?" he asked, extending one finger with each question.

"He's gorgeous. And he's got a great personality. From what he's shown me so far, I think he's a good person, but I don't know him that well. I met him a month ago, and we had sex twice. He's had a vasectomy, and I'm on the pill. Imagine that."

"He doesn't sound like someone who doesn't do relationships. He sounds like someone who wants to protect his child from heartbreak."

I hadn't looked at it that way, but after he mentioned it, it made perfect sense. "I hadn't thought of that."

"So, what did he say? When you told him?"

"That's just it. I haven't told him."

His eyes went wide. "What? You're not serious?"

"That's why I'm here. I need to decide what to do."

He cocked his head to the side, and did the eyebrow thing. "Are you considering *not* telling him?"

My eyes dropped. "Uh huh."

He wagged his finger at me as if scolding me. "You didn't conceive this child alone. You owe it to him – and to the child – to tell him."

His response made sense. It wasn't what I'd hoped for, but I couldn't argue his with his logic.

"Okay. I'll see if he'll meet me and have a talk."

"Is everything friendly between you two?"

"Well," I said. "That's where things get sticky."

TEN

Smokey

I started riding a motorcycle when I was 18 years old, and never looked back. I found it satisfying for many reasons, the main one being the sense of freedom I felt when I had the wind in my face. Having been charged with the task of mentoring a prospect changed everything. In one afternoon, riding went from an escape to being a pain in my ass.

We rolled into the shop and came to a stop, with Tank parking twenty feet ahead of me. I pulled off my helmet and hopped off the bike in fluid motion.

Tank pulled off his helmet, and turned to face me. "I don't understand--"

I took a few steps in his direction. "That's the problem, *prospect*. You don't fucking understand. You're a prospect. You want to be an outlaw biker, but you're *not* one. I am. *You* listen to *me*. Like it or fucking not, I'm in charge of this clusterfuck, and you're along for the God damned ride."

He lifted his leg over the tank, brushed his hands against the thighs of his jeans, and looked at me. He did a pretty poor job of hiding his regret, but I didn't give a fuck. I wasn't going to let up on him one bit.

Not now, not ever.

If it was my job to train him how to be a Filthy Fucker, he was going to be the best the club had to offer when he went from prospect to patch.

"I'll quit fucking around. I'm sorry."

Out of the corner of my eye, I saw Crip approaching. He stopped behind my bike, crossed his arms, and waited. After taking a few more steps toward Tank, I paused. I took a long hit off my vape, stared blankly at him while I savored the taste, and then blew the cloud to the side.

"When you were in the Corps, did you march like a fucking slob, going wherever you wanted, while the rest of the Marines marched in formation?" I asked.

He shook his head. "No, Sir."

"What would have happened if you did?"

"I'd have been written up."

"Called on the carpet, and then punished, right?"

He nodded. "Yes, Sir."

"When there were two of you going somewhere, did you have a procedure, or did you just nonchalantly walk?"

I knew the answers to the questions I asked, I was the son of a Marine. Knowing allowed me to ask the right questions, make valid points, and not sound like an idiot in the process.

"If there were two of us, we walked everywhere *in step.*"

"You walked side by side. His left foot went forward, your left foot went forward. His right, your right, correct?"

"Yes, Sir."

"In the army, they walk around with their hands in their pockets. One soldier walking at one speed, and the other just slobbing along at another speed. Did you know that?"

He nodded. "I've seen them."

"Which looks better?"

"The Marines."

"They look organized, right? Side by side, going everywhere at the same pace. They look like they're marching, even if they're walking to the store."

He nodded. "Yes, Sir."

"We do the same fucking thing here, *prospect*. It makes us look organized. When there's two of us, we ride two abreast. Always. Any more of that hotdogging shit will get your ass written up. Believe me, I'm keeping track."

"It won't happen again."

"Did Meat let you do that shit?"

He didn't respond. Hell, he didn't need to. I could tell by the look on his face that Meat didn't give a shit. At least Tank wasn't the type to snitch Meat out.

"You're not riding with him anymore," I said, my tone stern. "I won't put up with an ounce of your shit, understand?"

"Yes, Sir."

I shook my head. "How long you been out of the Marines?"

"A little over a year."

"How long was your basic training? The amount of time it took you to go from civilian to Marine?"

"Thirteen weeks, Sir."

"Thirteen weeks?" I nodded as if he'd revealed something I was unaware of. "Well, guess what? Your training here is 52 fucking weeks. That ought to give you an idea of how cautious we are of letting the wrong motherfucker wear our patch. Our training is longer than the Marines, and we spend most of that extra time weeding out the fucktards, understand?"

He gave a sharp nod. "Yes, Sir."

"That's another thing. Call me sir again, and I'll put a bullet in your thigh. We'll change your name from Tank to Gimp. Got it?"

"Yes, S--" His eyes fell to the floor. He let out a sigh, and then he looked up. "What do I call you?"

"Smoke. Smokey. Or, Boss." I grinned at the thought of him calling me Boss. "Yeah, let's go with Boss. I like that. Forget the other two. Call me Boss."

"Yes, Boss."

I liked the sound of it.

"I thought *I* was the boss," Crip said from behind me.

I glanced over my shoulder. "You're the boss of all *patched* members. He's a fucking *prospect*, and damned poor one at that. I'm Boss, as far as he's concerned, until I say otherwise."

Crip gave a nod. "Fair enough."

"Got a minute?" Crip asked.

I lifted my chin slightly, and made eye contact with Tank. "Go count the fence posts out in the parking lot, prospect. Twice."

"Yes, Boss."

As Tank walked toward the parking lot, Crip turned toward me and chuckled. "See? All that shit you were asking him? It's shit he can relate to."

"Gotta speak a subordinate's language," I said. "Just like talking to a child. You gotta speak to 'em in a language they can understand."

He watched Tank saunter toward the fence, and then looked at me. "Why were you riding his ass? What was he doing?"

"We were coming up the 5 from Encinitas, and the dipshit kept riding out ahead of me. Hell, I was going 90, who fucking knows how fast he was going. Lost sight of him a few times."

"What the fuck?" His eyes thinned. "You need to put a stop to that shit."

I shot him a sideways look. "Motherfucker, did you just listen to our conversation? I *did* put a stop to that shit."

"I'm not pissed off at you, I'm just pissed." He swung the toe of his boot against a pebble, and kicked it across the shop floor. "Just got off the phone. They indicted Meathead."

"Bad?"

"Felon in possession. Firearm in furtherance of a crime. Gave him the RICO act with the last charge, which was some bullshit about the guy being black. Said it was a hate crime."

"That's bullshit," I said. "White, black, brown, or yellow. Meat hated all motherfuckers equal."

"Agreed. The ATF brought charges against him. Impossible to fight those pricks."

"Motherfucker." I took a hit off my vape and shook my head. "And, I thought my day was going bad."

He pointed toward my bike. "Phone's ringing."

I turned away. "Probably Cholo. Got three jobs coming up."

Surprised to see it was Sandy calling, I considered not answering, then swiped my thumb across the screen and raised the phone to my ear. "This is Smokey."

"Smokey, this is Sandy. We need to uhhm. We need to talk."

The tone of her voice alone made my asshole pucker. Visions of her telling me I needed to go get a Z-Pak to cure something came to mind.

"Whatever it is, you can say it over the phone."

"No. We need to talk in person."

"Anything you need to say can be said over the phone."

"We need to meet in person, really."

I hated to be a prick, but I had to. I enjoyed her company too much. If I met her in person, it'd be a matter of minutes and I'd be fucking her – or wanting to, anyway. I knew me well enough to know if I started again, stopping would be impossible.

"Not gonna happen. You can either say what it is you have to say, or I'm going to hang up."

She sighed into the receiver. *"Fine. I hope you're on stable ground."*

Prepared to learn what strain of disease I needed to prepare to rid myself of, I cocked my head to the side, made eye contact with Crip, and waited.

"I'm pregnant. And, I know what you're going to ask, so I'll answer it first. Yes, it's yours."

"Hello?"

"Hello?"

"Smoke? Are you there?"

ELEVEN

Sandy

My throat went dry on the way to answer the door. I reached for the knob, paused, and pressed my tongue to the roof of my mouth. Satisfied I'd at least be able to say *hi,* I pressed my eye against the peephole, even though I knew it was him.

A fish-eyed view of his handsome face and broad shoulders caused my stomach to sink. Talking to him wasn't something I wanted to do, it was something I must. It was what was right.

But it was going to hurt.

I pulled the door open.

He stood in the breezeway with a plastic bag hanging from his left hand, and his right thumb resting against the top of his belt. His mouth slowly curled into a smirk.

I must have stared for longer than I thought, because he cleared his throat and reminded me that I hadn't invited him in or stepped out of the doorway.

He took half a step back and looked at me. "I might have been confused. You wanted me to come *here*, right?"

"Uh huh."

He nodded his head toward me. "You want me to duck under your arm, or are you going to move?"

RIGID

I released the door handle and stepped to the side. "Come in."

He walked past me. With each step, the plastic bag swung wildly – a result of his bravado swagger. I looked him up and down as he sauntered toward the living room, wishing for that fleeting moment that everything was different between us, but knowing it never would be.

He sat down on the couch as if it was something he'd done a thousand times. He lifted the bag to his lap, and as he fumbled to get something from it, the girl in me interrupted his plan.

"What's in the bag?"

He paused with his hand buried deep in the bag, and chuckled. "Couldn't wait another fifteen seconds, could you?"

I sat down on the loveseat across from him. "No."

He pulled out a book, stood, and extended his hand. "A book."

Surprised, I reached for it nonetheless. "You brought me a book?"

"*What to Expect When You're Expecting*," he said. "Best book there is for a pregnant woman."

It wasn't at all what I expected. I figured he brought a sandwich, some bananas, or maybe an ice cream. A box of condoms as some sick joke seemed his speed, but not something motherly. I looked at the tattered cover, opened it, and quickly realized as I thumbed through the dog-eared and highlighted pages that the book was well-used.

I met his gaze, all the while struggling to contain my emotions. "Thank you."

"I'd appreciate it if you take care of it." He waved his hand toward the book. "It's got sentimental value."

"Was it yours?"

He relaxed into the seat and nodded a few times, lightly. "It *is* mine. I'm letting you read it."

I felt offended and privileged at the same time. "Oh."

"It was Christine's."

Great. He'd given me the book that his former skank had before she gave birth and then took off. I set it to the side, and then pushed it as far away as I could. "Uhhm. Thanks."

He gazed down at his lap. While I prepared to begin what was sure to be a long conversation, he beat me to the punch.

"We'd read it every night. Probably read that damned thing half a dozen times if I read it once. I highlighted the important stuff, but don't just read what I've got marked, it's all useful."

"She's your ex? Christine?"

Still staring into his lap, he nodded. "Eddie's mom. Yeah."

"Where is she now?" I asked, my tone almost snide.

"She died."

I seemed to do a pretty good job of making myself out to be an idiot in his presence. I cleared my throat, swallowed hard, and then offered an apology. "I'm so sorry."

"Yeah, me too. I know at some point you'll ask, and I don't ever want it brought up in front of Eddie, so I'll just tell you now." He lifted his gaze to meet mine. "She died of a heroin overdose the day we got home from the hospital. She was clean the entire pregnancy, but didn't last a day after Ed was born. Never did figure out where she got it, but it doesn't matter much." He shook his head, and then his eyes fell to his lap. "Addiction's a bitch."

I felt sick. "I thought. She uhhm. Wow. I'm sorry. Really."

He shrugged, but didn't speak.

"You said you had a daughter, right?"

He looked up. "Yeah. Her name's Eddie."

"Is it short for something?"

"Short for Eddie Cassandra Wallace."

I smiled. My first name was Cassandra, but I wasn't going to tell him. At least not yet. "I like it. A lot."

His eyes widened just a little. "Which part of it?"

"All of it."

He smiled a dimple producing smile. Seeing it all but melted me.

I was on a roll, so I pushed on. "What's your name?"

"Grayson Edward Wallace. Middle name's my father's. First is his father's. It's a family thing."

"I like it. So, you named your daughter after your father?"

"Yep."

I folded my arms under my boobs and hugged myself tight. "I'm scared, Smokey."

"It's not going to be that bad," he said.

I shot him a look. "How can you say that?"

"Been a while," he said. "But I remember most of it. It's not bad until the very end. Well, the puking is the shits. If you get the morning sickness, that is. Not bad, other than that--"

"Raising a child alone? You know a little bit about that, don't you? I'd think you'd be a little more sympathetic," I said.

He leaned forward and scrunched his nose. "What the fuck are you talking about?

I spread my arms wide and glanced down at my non-existent stomach. "This."

"Oh, you're doing it alone, are you?"

His response came so quickly it confused me. I hesitated for a moment, and recalled exactly what I had said, and how he responded. I decided I hadn't made myself clear, and that I needed to take a different approach. "I have no one. I'm not going back to New Mexico to live with my aunt and--"

He stood, folded his arms across his chest and shot me a glare. "Whoa. Hold on. I'm not walking out on my kid, if that's what you're thinking. Stone cold sober, we both made the decision to fuck. It was a risk we took, and this is the result. Now, we're going to get through it, together. One way or another."

With my eyes fixed on his, I stared back at him, and blinked. Slowly. "Are you saying--"

"I'm saying I went to the doctor, and the he said my fucking vasectomy is dicked up. I'm saying I've done the single parent thing, and it ain't worth a shit. I'm saying watching a kid grow up wondering what it would be like to have the other parent in the picture isn't a pretty sight. I'm saying we need to figure out a way to try and make something work. And, I guess, I'm saying I'm willing."

I should have been flattered or grateful, but, oddly, I wasn't. I was fully prepared for him to get mad and stomp out, leaving me to make all the decisions – and raise the child – alone. His acceptance of the situation we were in wasn't at all what I was expecting, and as much as I should have, I didn't like it.

"We don't really know each other. I mean. You can't say you love me." I looked him up one side and down the other, and although he looked amazing, I tried to act as if I found him repulsive. "I *know* I don't love you. I mean. You're cool and everything, but--"

"Fuck no, I don't love you," he snapped back. "Hell, I don't even *know* you. But that doesn't mean we can't try and make something work. Our child doesn't need to be punished, that's for sure. He or she, whichever it is, deserves to grow up with *both* parents."

"Two parents that don't love each other?"

With his arms still folded in front of his chest, he shrugged. "We might end up in love someday."

I laughed. "Really? How's that work?"

He glared at me. "Fuck, I don't know. We get to know each other, then we fall in love. I'm no fucking expert. People do it all the time."

"They get to know each other, fall in love, have sex, get married, and *then* have kids."

"Well, your little fantasy world got fucked up when you were riding my cock in the kitchen, and I don't know what to tell you. All I know for sure is this: I watched Eddie cry herself to sleep at night on and off from the time she was five until she was eleven. I wouldn't wish that pain on any child. So, maybe we do all the shit you're talking about, we just do it out of order. But they're still the same fucking steps."

I stood and stared at him blankly. I was speechless. I collapsed onto the couch. My chest tightened, and all but suffocated me. I lowered my head into my hands and began to cry. I had no idea what I wanted, and I was an emotional wreck. While I sat there and wept, I felt the couch give as he took a seat beside me.

His arm slid across my shoulders.

Then, pulled me into him. "Don't cry," he whispered.

I rested my head on his shoulder, uncertain of why I was so emotional. As his hands began to softly rub my back, I realized, at least for that moment, that I wasn't alone.

And, I liked it.

TWELVE

Smokey

Be careful what you wish for. I'd said that phrase so many times over the years that it had all but become a mantra. Now, I could look in the mirror and say it to the man looking back at me.

I'd spent every day since Eddie's birth wishing her mother had lived, and that we could have had the opportunity to raise our child in a two-parent home. Yearning for a slice of normalcy, yet knowing it would never be, every day I wished Eddie could have a life similar to most of her friends. The thought of her being abandoned by a stepmother prevented me from being serious with anyone over the last sixteen years, leaving her mother, Christine, as my last relationship.

If I could call it that.

It was the longest one night stand in the history of mankind. The wend result was the best thing that ever happened to me even if it didn't go how I'd hoped. Now, fate comes knocking on my door once again, and my wishes are granted.

Kind of.

I'd wanted the ability to raise a child in a family setting. Much to my surprise, my prayers had been answered with Sandy's pregnancy. Embracing the situation, however, required going against the grain of a lifetime of efforts to protect Eddie from harm.

But I had to do what was right.

We sat in a local coffee shop talking as if we'd just met.

I took a sip of coffee, pushed the cup aside, and studied her. She was a gorgeous woman, if she was nothing else.

"You're walking through the grocery store parking lot, and there's a wallet in front of you. You bend down, pick it up, and open it. Twelve $100 bills, and a handwritten note is all that's inside. No ID, no credit cards, nothing. The note says, *Apple juice, graham crackers*, and *bananas*. That's it. What do you do?"

She grinned. "Where do you come up with this shit?"

"My vault. Answer the question."

"I load my groceries in my car, lock it, and then go to the customer service counter, and turn it in."

I nodded. "Good answer."

"Why does the note say those things? Apple juice, graham crackers, and bananas?"

I shrugged. "They're things a kid would eat. I was trying to tug at your subconscious heart strings a little."

"Oh."

She twisted her mouth to the side and gazed down at the table. After a moment, she looked up. "What if the baby's a boy. Eighteen years down the road, are you going to encourage him to ride in a club?"

"Nope."

"Why not?"

"It's not a place for everyone. If he decides on his own that that's what he wants, so be it. He'll get no influence from me."

"You're his father. He'll admire you. He'll naturally want to follow in your footsteps."

I widened my eyes. "Who says I'll still be in a club when he's old enough to make decisions?"

"So, you'll quit, or whatever?"

"Maybe."

"Oh. Okay."

"Favorite album?"

She chuckled. "I thought you were going to say color."

"I'm only asking important shit. Favorite album?"

"How can my favorite album be important?"

I glared at her in disbelief. "The type of music you listen to defines who you are. Okay, instead of favorite, if you were stuck on a fucking island, and you were going to be there for two years before anyone rescued you, what one album – if you could only have one – would you have with you?"

She twisted a lock of hair with her index finger and gazed down at the floor. After taking a few drinks of her coffee, she stopped fucking with her hair and looked up. "I don't know. What about you?"

"Rolling Stones, *Sticky Fingers*."

"Don't know it," she said.

I grinned. "You will."

She hoisted her coffee, appeared to realize it was empty, and set it aside.

"Want another?" I asked.

"No thank you. I'm full." She appeared to be preoccupied in thought, so I let her be. After a moment, she focused on me. "I think maybe Maroon Five, *It Won't Be Soon Before Long*."

"The album?"

"Uh huh."

"Do you like Coldplay?"

She shrugged. "I mean. I don't know. Kind of, but not--"

"You've said enough."

"Why?" she asked. "Do you?"

"No, and if you did, I was going to leave. Coldplay's a deal breaker."

She laughed. "Really?"

"Yep."

She chuckled, and then seemed to have an epiphany. "If you could meet anyone, dead or alive, and go to lunch with them, who would it be, and what would you say?" she blurted.

"Good one," I said. "Let me think."

After a moment, I met her gaze. "Kennedy. JFK. I'd tell him not to go down Elm Street."

She looked surprised. "Why?"

"I think he would have made a great president. Things might be different now if he would have stayed in office. Same question to you."

"That's easy," she said. "Doris Day."

My jaw dropped. "Doris Day?"

"Uh huh."

"What the fuck? Really?"

She grinned and nodded eagerly as if truly satisfied she'd given the answer she wanted to. "She was always smiling, and her smile is infectious. Every time I see her movies, I either smile or cry, and her movies are awesome. *Pillow Talk*? Oh my God, that was so good. And *Send Me No Flowers*? *Lover Come Back*? *Move Over darling*? They were awesome. And *Please Don't Eat the Daisies*? Yeah. It'd be Doris Day for me."

"What would you say to her?"

"*Thank you*. That's it. I'd just say thanks for making me smile."

Her blonde hair normally hung straight down over her shoulders. She'd fixed it differently, and it was fixed into a mass of curls, leaving it not near as long, but twice as big. I studied it, and wondered just how much time she spent making it that way.

After deciding she must have spent an hour doing it, my focus went from her hair to her face. With her elbow resting on the edge of the table, and her cheek against her fist, she seemed to be daydreaming.

I let her sit there for a moment, lost in whatever she was thinking of. When her eyes appeared to focus again, I grinned. "I like your hair. It's different today."

"I made it big. I like big hair. Well, sometimes."

"I like it, too."

She made the "O" face, and then rapped her knuckles against the table. "What do you eat on a hot dog?"

"Mustard and relish," I said flatly. Anything else is sacrilegious."

She shook her head. "I disagree."

I was curious to hear what she had to say about my favorite comfort food. She didn't know it, but she picked the wrong guy to fuck with about hot dogs. "What do *you* eat on them?"

"Sport peppers and chili."

"Good answer." It was the only answer she could have provided that I would have accepted as being remotely close to proper. "Ever eat 'em with ketchup?"

She scrunched her nose. "I don't even eat it on French fries."

"No shit? What do you dip 'em in?"

"Horseradish sauce and barbeque."

"No shit. Makes eating 'em at McDonald's tough, huh?"

"Nope." She reached for her purse, stuck her hand inside, and after a digging around, pulled out a fistful of horseradish packets. "I keep these in my purse."

"You keep fucking horseradish sauce in your purse?"

She tossed the packets in her bag. "I get it at Arby's. Every time I'm in there I get about fifty of them."

I nodded toward her purse. "What else you got in there?"

She dumped it onto the table and grinned.

Surprised at her willingness to dump her life onto the table, I sifted through the pile. A wallet. iPod. A dozen packets of horseradish. A red bikini bottom. A flip-top box of gum. Fingernail clippers. Earbuds. A pair of sunglasses. Three pens. Hand sanitizer. Lip gloss. A phone. A fingernail file. Car keys complete with pepper spray. Lipstick. Three different colors of fingernail polish. A folding pocketknife. A red bikini top. Three sleeves of takeout chopsticks. Numerous gum wrappers.

"Quite an assortment."

She shrugged. "I just cleaned it."

"Didn't bother putting the bikini or the chopsticks up?"

She reached for the chopsticks and shook her head. "I always have chopsticks."

"Why?"

"In case I need to eat something, and there aren't any."

I was fascinated. "Do you eat everything with them?"

"Anything I can pick up. Not hamburgers or hotdogs, but a lot of other things."

I found her response, and her affinity for the wooden sticks, cute.

"What about the bikini?"

"In case I want to lay in the sun."

"You just hop into it, huh?"

"Uh huh."

"Change in your car?"

"Wherever. The beach. My car. Whatever."

I nodded toward her keys. "What are you going to do with that can of Mace?"

"Spray someone."

"Like who?"

She reached for it as if offended. "Whoever nabs me."

"Are they after you?" I asked, stone-faced. "The men in the black helicopters?"

"Don't be a dick. I'm a girl. Men try to snatch us all the time. If someone tries, I'm going to spray them. Or, cut them with that knife."

"That'll just piss 'em off. I'll show you how to use a gun. Put a bullet in their chest and they'll let go every time."

"I don't have a gun."

"You will."

"I don't know if I could--"

"I'll teach you how to use one."

She put the car keys in her purse, and then sighed. "I run everywhere at night. I'm always scared someone's going to get me. I run from store to my car. I run in and out of the gas station. I run in and out of the club. Everywhere."

"How often do you go to the club?"

"Oh, I work at one."

I took a sip of the lukewarm coffee. "I thought you were a waitress at the fish place? With Lex?"

"I am. But I work at the Main Attraction, too."

I choked on my coffee. "The strip club?"

"Uh huh."

I shook my head. "Not anymore, you don't."

She cocked her head to the side and stared. "Excuse me?"

"I want you to quit."

"And when did you start telling me what to do?"

"If we're going to try and make this work, we've got to have some ground rules. You working at a strip club isn't good for the baby, for you, or for me."

"I need the money."

"I've got plenty of money."

She shook her head. "I need it to pay my rent. Sometimes the restaurant, especially in the off season--"

I turned my palm to face her. "Just stop. That's another thing we were going to talk about. I need to talk to Eddie, but I was thinking. Maybe in like two weeks. How about you move in?"

She stared at me with wide eyes and an open mouth. "Huh?'

"Move in," I said. "Being pregnant ain't easy, especially if you're alone. Doctor's appointments, being sick, and once you get to six or seven months--"

"Move in? You and me? Together?"

I nodded. "What else did you think we were going to do? Share custody or something stupid? You get the kid one week, me the next?"

"I didn't--"

"Look," I said. "In case I didn't make myself clear before, I want to try and make this work. You and me. Relationship. Learn to live with each other. Have a baby. Raise it together. Have a family."

She squinted and then stared. "But we don't love each other."

"Maybe we will in time."

She appeared to accept my response. After a moment's thought, she raised her index finger. "First rule. No other women. Ever. Not one. No excuses. If you ever cheat, me and the baby are gone."

I shrugged. "No problem, I don't cheat. My first rule. Quit the strip club."

"Okay."

I made a fist and held it over the center of the table.

She looked at it, and then at me. She clenched her hand into a fist, and pounded it into mine.

On that day, in the coffee shop, we made a pact.

An agreement.

I found it exciting in many respects.

Well, all except for one.

Telling Eddie.

THIRTEEN

Sandy

I knocked on the doorframe, and waited out of sight of the open door.

He cleared his throat. "Who is it?"

"Sandy," I said. "Texxxas."

"Come in."

I stepped through the door and looked around. Mr. Rosetti's office didn't look like it belonged inside a strip club. Unlike the rest of the club, it was well lit, brightly painted, and decorated with modern office furniture.

Mr. Rosetti was nice, and not at all a weirdo or a pervert like everyone who didn't know him assumed. He was a businessman, and looked at the club as a business, and at the women who worked there as his employees.

He pointed to one of the three open chairs. "Have a seat."

It was my day off, but I doubted he realized it. Dressed in my street clothes, and feeling kind of out of place, I glanced at the chair, and then at him, and sat down.

He peered over the top of his glasses. "Is everything alright?"

I hugged my purse. "Oh, yeah. Just fine, thank you."

He removed his glasses, and set them aside. "Are you sure?"

He was the best boss one could ever ask for, and was the most understanding man ever. He even remembered each of the girl's birthdays, and passed out cards with $100 in them to celebrate. I felt terrible giving him the news, and struggled with just what to say.

"I uhhm. I need to. I have to quit."

He went bug-eyed. "Quit? What? Where are you going?"

"Nowhere. Just going home."

"Don't quit. You don't want to do that. It's never a good idea."

"I need to, really. I just wanted to let you know. You've been good to me, and I don't want to leave on bad terms."

"You can't go anywhere and make this kind of money, Sandy. Take a few days off, and think about it. I'm sure you'll come to your senses. You sure there's nothing you want to talk about?"

I clutched my purse and rocked back and forth in the seat. "No. Not really. And, no, I don't need to think about it. I just need to go ahead and quit."

"I'll give you 70% of the cut from the drinks, and 100% from your take on private dances. How's that?"

It made me wish I would have threatened to quit two years prior. At those rates, I'd easily make another $100-150 nightly.

"I really can't."

"What's wrong? Did Joe Marcelli approach you? From San Diego? Are you going to San Diego?"

I shook my head. "I'm pregnant."

He inhaled a deep breath, held it, and then exhaled. "You've got a while before you'll need to quit. Just stick around until you're uncomfortable, and then--"

"I'm sorry, I can't. The father has asked that I quit."

He nodded toward the door. "Not one of my employees?"

"Oh. No. He's someone else."

He stood, and then clasped his hands together. "Give me two weeks. How about that? Two weeks? It'll let me find someone to replace you in the headlines. It's not easy getting someone that'll draw the crowds you do."

Two weeks would let me stick a few thousand dollars away, and I was sure it'd be that long before I moved in with Smokey anyway, if not longer.

"I'll agree to it if you keep those rates you were talking about. 100% of my dances, and 70% of drinks."

"I can do that."

I stood. "Okay. I'll stay two weeks."

"Thank you. And, before you go, be sure and come say goodbye. I'll miss you, Sandy. I really will."

"I'll miss you too, Mr. Rosetti."

I smiled and turned toward the door.

Two more weeks.

What could that hurt?

FOURTEEN

Smokey

I rolled up beside the three other bikes, came to a stop, and then whacked the throttle twice. Standing on the far side of the shop, Crip cupped his hands to his ears and shot me a glare. I shut off the motor and grinned.

As I was hanging my helmet on the handlebars, he shouted across the shop. "God damn it with you and that loud ass bike. Shut it down at the street and roll in here from now on with that loud cocksucker off. I've only asked you what? A thousand times?"

"I'll try and remember," I yelled, turning to face him as I spoke. "Got a lot on my mind."

He shook his head and turned toward Pee Bee.

"The Nut will be here in a minute." I took a few steps in their direction. "Wanting to talk to the four of you."

Cholo, Pee Bee, and Crip were all gathered around the refrigerator. I'd sent each of them a text message to see if they were at the shop, and after finding that they were, asked P-Nut to come in as well.

I wanted to tell them about the changes I was going to go through before they heard it from someone else. It seemed anytime information came from anywhere other than the source, it was inaccurate at best.

Bikers with Ol' Ladies were looked at differently than bikers who were single. Often, when a man like me ended up in a relationship, he was looked down upon and considered a *sellout*. If the four men I was speaking to accepted my situation, everyone else would do the same. Convincing them I was doing what was right should be easy, as three of them had Ol' Ladies.

"So, what the fuck's going on?" Crip asked. "Having problems with the prospect?"

I pulled my vape from my pocket and checked the battery life. "Nope. In fact, he's coming along smartly."

"Why the meeting?" he asked.

I took a long hit off the vape. "Is that what this is?"

He glanced at Pee Bee and Cholo, and then looked at me. "Looks like it."

I blew the cloud of smoke toward Crip. "Makes you nervous when someone other than you calls a few of the fellas together, huh?"

"God damn it, Smokey. What'd I tell you about that fucking thing? Blow that shit somewhere else."

"My bad, Crip. Shit, I can't remember a God damned thing. Think the exhaust fumes are getting to me. Either that or the adhesive from all the tile work."

He glared. "I mean it."

I extended my fist toward Peeb. After he pounded it, I did the same with Cholo. Then, I made eye contact with Crip and gave him a half-hearted nod.

He shook his head and turned away.

Aggravating him was part of what made being around him so much fun. Most of the fellas knew I was full of shit, and simply accepted me as being me. Crip took everything personal, and genuinely let me get under his skin. The fact that I could irritate him enough to get him off his game drove me to do so even more.

After two minutes of silence, Crip turned to face me. "What's this about?"

"Got some news to give ya."

He folded his arms across his chest. "Well, give it."

I took another hit off my vape, and held the smoke in. "Waiting on the Nut."

He shook his head. "Perfect. That's all I need is the two of you together."

"We're all brothers, *Brother*," I said, my tone sarcastic.

P-Nut was a veteran with the Fuckers, and was a lot like me. He was a man of principle, had a good set of moral values, and didn't take shit from anyone, especially Crip. He didn't hang with Pee Bee or Cholo, and not because they didn't like him. It was more a result of his desire to survive on a day-to-day basis without being scrutinized by anyone.

He would do anything for the club, for his brothers, or for a good cause, as long as he was the one to make the decision.

And, it was that lone wolf attitude that kept him and Crip at odds.

The sound of a motorcycle's approaching exhaust caused me to tense. I wasn't necessarily nervous about talking to them, but I wasn't completely comfortable either. After spending nearly two decades screwing every woman who held still long enough for me to poke my cock in them, settling down and having a baby with someone would certainly raise eyebrows, and I knew it.

P-Nut came screaming through the parking lot at twice the speed that was safe and shot past the shop. Beyond the opening of the overhead door, but still well within our view, he locked up his rear brake and slid into a smoky 180 degree turn.

RIGID

With his front tire now facing the garage door and the motorcycle still well into a power-slide, he hit the throttle and launched the bike into the shop.

Blazing across the floor – and directly toward us – at full speed, his little display of power didn't bother me. Crip, on the other hand, was screaming at the top of his lungs.

P-Nut's bike came to a screeching stop right beside mine.

He revved the throttle once, and shut off the engine. After tossing his helmet onto the floor, he looked up and grinned. "That was *interesting*."

"God damn it, P-Nut," Crip hollered. "That was un-fucking-necessary."

P-Nut pulled a pack of cigarettes from his front pocket, lit one, and then looked at Crip through one eye while the other was pinched shut. "Which part?"

"All of it," Crip snarled.

In the middle of taking a drag off his cigarette, P-Nut paused, and then blew the smoke to the side.

"Can't agree with you on that, Crip." He waved his hand toward the wide-open garage door. "Fast as I was going, I had to shoot past the door, or I'd have wrecked. Then, if I didn't do that little U-turn, I'd have hit the far side of the fucking fence. And, the coming in the shop part? Shit, you know I ride hard. Nope. I'm thinking pretty much all of it was necessary."

He took long strides across the shop floor. Upon reaching us, he pounded my fist, and then gave Pee Bee and Cholo a nod. "What's up fellas?"

"You need to slow that piece of shit down," Crip said. "If you'd have been going the fucking speed limit, we wouldn't be having this conversation, would we?"

P-Nut flicked his ash on the floor, rubbed it with the toe of his boot, and then looked up. "Changin' the name of the club to the *Clean Clan* or are we keeping the *Filthy Fuckers* patch on our colors?"

Crip glared.

P-Nut shrugged. "Just wondering. I mean, if we're all going to abide by the speed limits and everything. Want me to turn in my pistol, too? I could start carrying a bible and a box of Snickers bars instead of a pistol and a pack of cigarettes."

Crip clenched his jaw. "Slow the fuck down in the parking lot."

P-Nut took a long drag off his cigarette, blew the smoke in Crip's direction, and then began to rock back and forth on the balls of his feet. "Got all the decision makers in the same place. Hope nobody drops a bomb, this club would be brainless."

The Nut never stood still for longer than a few seconds, and to those that didn't know him, he seemed sketchy and nervous. His given name was Percy, and considering the fact he acted nuts most of the time, he earned the name P-Nut.

"Shouldn't take long," I said "I've just got something I need to bring to light."

"Make it quick," Crip said with a laugh. "He's making me nervous."

Although every member of the club was my brother, I didn't look at them all the same. I'd put my life on the line for any of them, or I wouldn't have taken the oath to become a Filthy Fucker. Being close friends with each of them, however, was impossible.

The four men in front of me were ones that mattered to me the most.

"I've got something to say, and I'd appreciate it if you keep your shitty remarks to yourselves."

RIGID

Cholo, Pee Bee, and Crip were all leaning against the workbench, while P-Nut nervously paced the floor between them and the far wall.

"You all know that I've got a daughter, and that I'm protective of her. I've got--"

P-Nut stopped pacing and shot me a look of concern. "Nobody fucked with Eddie, did they? God damn it, I'll kill a motherfucker--"

"Settle down, Nut. No. Eddie's fine. Hear me out."

He lit another cigarette, and went right back to pacing the floor.

"In the last month, I've been seeing a girl." I figured saying I'd been *seeing* her would sound a lot better than saying we'd fucked twice. I scanned the men for reactions, and other than Nut's pacing, everyone seemed pretty calm, so I continued. "And I liked spending time with her, but I knew it'd never amount to much with my rule about relationships and all."

I paused, took a long pull on my vape, and then tilted my head toward the ceiling. After exhaling the smoke into the steel structure of the shop, I lowered my gaze and dropped the bomb.

"She's pregnant."

P-Nut stopped in his tracks and looked right at me. One of his eyebrows arched.

The other three men's jaws dropped.

While Crip's mouth twisted into a shitty smirk, I continued. "And, before any of you say anything slick, she'll be moving in with me. We're having the baby. Together."

Crip rubbed his face with the palms of his hands and then crossed his arms. "Going domestic on us, huh?"

"Nope. Just doing what's right."

"It's good you're doing right by her," Cholo said. "She's good people.

The two of you can come over and stare at the beach with Lex and me from the back deck. I mean it, Brother."

Crip shot him a look. "You know this chick?"

Cholo nodded. "Works with Lex."

I turned toward P-Nut. Standing in the same spot, he stood statue-still with his eyes fixed on the floor. Every few seconds, he'd blink.

"You alright, Nut?"

Without looking up, he nodded.

I nodded in return, giving him the time and space he needed to come to terms with the change. I looked at Pee bee. "Well?"

He shrugged and gave me his signature grin. "Tegan and I been going skin on skin for a bit. I can't say shit."

"I don't even know how to operate a condom," Crip said. "It's just by the grace of God I don't have a kid."

I couldn't believe it. I lowered my vape and glared. "So, that's it? None of you fuckers are going to talk shit?"

P-Nut looked up. "What'd Eddie say?"

"Ain't talked to her yet."

"But you're going to, right? Not just move the chick in?"

"Fuck no," I said. "I'll talk to Ed about it. Jesus, Nut, you know me better than that."

His nodded, and then his eyes fell to the floor. After a long pause, he looked up and clapped his hands. "I'm good with it."

I looked at the other three men and shook my head. "Nothing? Not one slick ass comment from the rest of you?"

"What'd you expect?" Crip asked with a dry laugh. "You're an asshole. If anyone would have said anything, you'd have either threatened to fight 'em, pulled your fucking gun, or called 'em a no-good cocksucker."

I shrugged, and then took a hit off my vape. "Probably right."

"Right as fuck." He chuckled and then extended his hand. "Congratulations. I know how much Eddie means to you. I hope this one is just as enjoyable."

As the president of the MC, Crip was an arrogant prick. As a person, he was as solid as any man could be. The problem, if it was in fact a problem, was that he was almost always acting as the president of the club.

I shook his hand. "Appreciate ya."

"What's her name?" P-Nut asked.

"Sandy."

"White? Black? Mexican?" He looked at Cholo and then at me. "*Hispanic?* Tall? Short? Blonde? Brunette? Is she thick? What the fuck's she look like?" he asked in one breathless sentence.

"Blonde," I said. "I don't know. Five foot six or so. She's a little thing with big boobs."

He fumbled to get a cigarette from his pack. After lighting it and taking a drag, he exhaled the smoke to the side, and fixed his eyes on mine. "Cute as fuck? Like traffic-stoppin' cute?"

Uncertainty washed over me. Concern came right behind it. I crossed my arms. "Yeah."

"She work at the *Main Attraction?*"

It was a strip club most of the men went into, and I should have known it was going to come up sooner or later.

"She's putting in her notice. But yeah. That's her."

"Texxxas," he said. "That's her stage name. Nice girl. You said *Sandy*, then said *big tits*, and my brain went *ding ding*."

"Oh shit," Crip said.

I turned toward him.

Pee Bee's eyes were as wide as saucers.

I looked at Crip and lifted my chin slightly. "You know her?"

"Yep."

I shifted my eyes to Pee Bee.

He grinned. "That's an affirmative, Ghost Rider."

Cholo shook his head. "Never been in the place. Just know her through Lex."

"Any of you fuck with her?" I looked the men over, pushed my vape into my back pocket, and then crossed my arms. "Tell me now. I fucking mean it."

Four heads shook side to side.

I pursed my lips and nodded. "Any of the other fellas? That you know of?"

Crip shook his head. "She's all business. Doesn't fuck with guys from the club. Least not that I know of."

Hearing it was a relief. I hadn't given any thought to fact that the fellas might know her, but if I'd have taken a moment to think about it, I would have known. The club where she worked was a common hangout for the MC.

"Appreciate the honesty," I said.

I let out a sigh. I was pleased that everything went as good as it did with the fellas. I had my doubts my luck was going to continue with my next stop, though.

Eddie was going to be a tough sell.

FIFTEEN

Sandy

Lex and I were sunbathing on her deck. The back of her house faced the ocean, and had an unobstructed view of the water, which placed what I expected to be an emotional conversation in a very relaxing setting.

She took a drink of tea, and then tilted her head toward me. "It's really rare for a person to fall in love first and have sex later. Especially now. I mean, crap. Girls have apps on their phone to hook up with guys. Swipe right, swipe left. It's crazy. They hook up, and if they like it, they do it again. If they get along after that, they end up hanging out for a few months while they continue to have sex, and *then* they fall in love. Falling in love is the last step for millennials."

"Did you and Cholo fall in love first?"

She let out a sigh. "Yeah."

I sat up in my lounge chair and pushed my sunglasses up the bridge of my nose. "I *knew* it! You were just trying to make me feel better."

"I was not. It's true," she said. "You know, if you guys would have kept seeing each other, maybe you would have fallen in love. But, you got pregnant first. And, just like Adam says, *it is what it is*. You can't change it, Sandy. You can only learn to live with it. I don't know. Maybe be grateful that he's not being a dick about it."

"I *am* grateful."

"You don't sound like it."

"I think I'm…I don't know. Maybe I'm scared."

I hated to admit it, but I was scared, and I knew it.

"Of what?"

"Failure. Of us not making it."

She pulled off her sunglasses. "Because you didn't fall in love first?"

I nodded. "Uh huh."

She laughed and then raised her index finger. "I'm sorry. I shouldn't have laughed. But that's ridiculous." She sat up and turned to face me. "Do you trust him?"

"I do."

"Do you think he'll cheat?"

"No, I don't. He made that pretty clear. Until *this*." I waved my hands over my stomach. "He didn't do relationships. But he said he didn't cheat, and never would. I believe him."

"Okay. So, if you would have fallen in love with *whoever* – some other random guy – do you think that would have been an assurance that they'd be faithful? Because you fell in love first?"

I shrugged. "I guess not."

"If Smokey doesn't cheat, you guys can get through anything. Believe me." She shook her head lightly. "The problem isn't the lack of love. It really isn't. It's the baby. It's being pregnant."

"What do you mean?"

"If you weren't pregnant, and you were seeing Smokey, you know, dating or whatever. And after a while he asked you to move in, would you be scared?"

My response was immediate, and without thought. "No."

"Even if you weren't in love?"

"Scared? No, I don't think so. I'd probably just move in. I'd have nothing to lose. If it didn't work out, I'd move out."

"Okay. Now you're pregnant. He asks you to move in, and you're all flipping out over it. The difference is the baby. Act like you're not pregnant. Move in, settle into place, and before you know it, you'll be in love. Problem solved. But the lack of love doesn't change a thing. He cares enough about you to take care of the baby, and not to cheat on you. You're far better off than most women who *are* in love."

As much as I hadn't liked my friendships with girls in the past, I sure liked being friends with Lex. Being without a mother for so long, I'd forgotten how important the interaction with another girl could be. Throughout our friendship, her advice was well thought out and worthy of my consideration.

I sat up and smiled. "We can be pregnant together."

She rubbed her belly. "We don't have a choice."

I relaxed into the lounge, put on my sunglasses, and gazed out at the horizon. "You're right, we don't."

As I watched the waves repeatedly crash into the shore, I began to wonder if I would change things even if I could.

In no time, I decided I wouldn't.

It was at that moment that I realized I was ready to begin my journey to fall in love with Grayson Edward Wallace.

SIXTEEN

Smokey

P-Nut and I had ridden to San Diego and were rolling along the Mission Valley Freeway in slow-moving traffic.

"Exit 3B to Friars," I shouted.

With his helmet all but off his head, and the loose fitting strap dangling below his chin, he gave me a look through the yellow lenses of his glasses. "Where the fuck we going?"

"There's a fucking mall there," I shouted. "I need to get Eddie's gift."

He gave a nod, and within a few minutes, we got off the exit and rode to the mall. After following me into the parking garage, he looked at the various parked cars, which were all expensive imports, and then at me.

He tossed his helmet onto the concrete beside his bike and then looked up as a $250,000 Bentley Coupe passed by us.

"You sure we're in the right place, Brother?"

I nodded. "We're going to Tiffany & Company. I need to get Eddie a ring."

He spit out a laugh and raised his leg over his seat. "Oh, hell yes. I'm gonna like this."

"You need to behave," I warned.

He straightened his kutte. "If there's a hot bitch in there, I'm gonna try and fuck her."

I climbed off my bike. "Damn it, Nut. Just. Just try and act accordingly."

He flashed a cheesy grin. "Always do."

We sauntered toward a plexiglass enclosed map that was on display in the courtyard, and studied it.

"Right around the corner." He looked at me and raised his eyebrows. "By Louis Vuitton and Neiman Marcus. Yeah, this'll be fun."

"C'mon, Romeo," I said with a roll of my eyes.

Dressed in jeans, boots, and our kuttes, we walked to the store amidst several stares and a few dropped jaws. Upon reaching it, I turned toward P-Nut.

"I meant what I said."

"Best behavior." He gave a nod. "But I'm on the prowl."

Upon pushing the door open, we were met by a wide-eyed guard.

Dressed in a suit, and built like a linebacker, he gave an unassuming nod. "Welcome to Tiffany's."

"I'm looking for a ring for my daughter," I said. "Diamond."

"One of our associates will be with you promptly," he said.

I offered a silent nod of appreciation.

"One of our *associates,*" Nut whispered mockingly.

I narrowed my eyes and shot him a glare. "I meant it."

"Good afternoon, and welcome to Tiffany's. I'm Jennis. How can I help you?" someone said from behind me.

Peering over my shoulder, P-Nut's eyebrows raised slightly. "What's your name again?"

"Jennis."

"Spell it."

I turned around. A tall, pale, and very thin woman dressed in a navy skirt and blazer stood with her hands dangling at her sides. Her hair hung past her shoulders and draped over her chest like a sheet of crimson silk.

"J, e, n, n, i, s," she said.

"Oh, Jennis. Sorry, thought you said Janice," P-Nut said. "We're looking for a diamond ring."

"*I'm* looking for a diamond ring," I said.

She smiled and alternated glances between us. "An engagement ring? Or--"

"No," P-Nut said before she finished.

"Yes," I said.

She looked at him, and then at me. "Yes, or no?"

I nodded. "Yes."

"No," P-Nut said.

She grinned. "What's the purpose of the ring?"

"To cause anyone who encounters the person wearing it to think she's spoken for."

"*She* would be your wife? Girlfriend?" She leaned forward and then glanced over each shoulder. "Sidepiece?"

P-Nut chuckled. "What do you know about sidepieces?"

She raised her delicate hand to her mouth and grinned a sly grin. "I'll never tell."

"I'm an expert at getting sexy redheads to talk--"

I elbowed P-Nut and stepped between them. "It's for my daughter."

She turned to the side and took a long stride toward one of the many display cases. "You want to scare off the--"

"I'll scare them off once they come through the door," I said. "I want this to minimize the amount of them I'll have to scare."

"We have a few pieces that may interest you. How old is she?"

"Seventeen."

She stepped behind the case and turned to face us. "Oh, what a great age."

"Yep," P-Nut said. "Just a couple years older than you."

Jesus H. Christ.

"Oh stop," she said, doing the hand to the face thing again. "Please, you're going to make me blush."

P-Nut glanced over each shoulder, then reached for his zipper. "I'll make you blush."

I turned to the side and shot him a glare. "Damn it, Nut."

"You guys are such fun." She reached into the case and retrieved three rings. "We have the *Infinity Line*, the *Legacy Line*, and the--"

"I'm sorry," I said upon seeing the rings. "I want a solitaire. Something *big*. Maybe a carat or two."

Her thin lips formed a delicate "O", and she scooped up the rings.

"You don't want a solitaire for Eddie, Smoke. She'll look like a seventeen-year-old..." He paused and twisted his mouth to the side.

I arched an eyebrow. "A seventeen-year-old *what*?"

He looked at Jennis.

Her eyebrows raised slowly, and then her head tilted to the side. "Courtesan?"

"Excuse me?"

She flipped her hair over her shoulder, leaned forward, and rested her hands against her hips. "One would assume she's engaged. A young woman wearing such an engagement ring may be perceived as being a..." She let out a dramatic sigh. "Gold digger?"

P-Nut pursed his lips and nodded.

"Really?" I asked.

She shrugged.

"What do you suggest?"

"The Somerset, Schlumberger Daisy, maybe the Enchant Scroll." She raised her index finger. "I'll be right back."

She grinned a shallow grin and disappeared behind another jewelry case at the front of the store.

P-Nut looked at me. "I'm gonna shove that chick so full of cock that it dislocates her hips."

"No, you're not."

"The fuck you say. Who's stopping me?"

"Leave her alone, Nut. I need to get this ring bought."

"I ain't talking about doing it *now*. Buy your ring and watch the master at work."

I coughed a laugh. "The master?"

He nodded. "You know what they say about skinny red-heads, don't ya?"

"I'm drawing a blank."

"They've got tight pussies, and they dive on a cock like the homeless on a $100 bill."

I shook my head. "Where do you come up with this shit?"

"Well-known fact, Brother."

"Take a look at these." She placed four rings in front of us. "The Somerset, Daisy, Enchant, and the Five-Row Metro."

"Five-Row," P-Nut said.

I reached for the ring she called the five-row. It had five rows of diamonds around the complete circumference of the ring, and looked elegant.

"I like this one."

RIGID

She tilted her head to the side and smiled. "It's a beautiful ring."

As I admired the ring, P-Nut took a step back, raised his hand to his chin, and studied her. Her focus alternated back and forth between me and him as I studied the ring and he studied her.

I imagined Eddie wearing the ring, and how it would look. I smiled and nodded. "I'll take it."

She gave a nod. "Very well."

She looked at me and then glanced at P-Nut and grinned. "Do you have a question?"

His eyes looked up and down her wispy frame a few times. When he finished eye-fucking her, he fixed his eyes on hers. "Just thinking."

She genuinely seemed interested. "About?"

His eyes fell to her waist, paused, and then slowly rose to meet hers. "I'd rather not say."

She leaned over the counter. "My job is to help the customer. How can I help you if you won't enlighten me?"

He shook his head. "Don't want to turn your face the same color as your hair."

She straightened her stance, glanced over her right shoulder, and then shook her head. "I'm not easily embarrassed."

"Remember, *you asked*," he said.

She leaned over the edge of the counter, widened her eyes, and grinned.

P-Nut leaned forward, rested his elbows on the edge of the glass display, and locked eyes with her. "You're not married, but you're in a relationship you're not committed to. Sexually speaking, he doesn't satisfy you. You want him to take possession of you in the bedroom, but you're afraid to tell him. There's a long list of things you want him to

134

do, and he hasn't so much as tried one. In fact, none of your boyfriends have. Not really. You go from relationship to relationship, not because you're not committed, but because things *just don't work out.* Each time, you become more sexually frustrated, and you tell yourself the next time will be different. But it's not. Eventually the man breaks up with you because of some bullshit excuse, and you leave convinced it's your fault. Well, Jennis, I've got news for you. It's not your fault. You just need to find the right man."

He took a step back, folded his arms across his chest, and grinned. "How'd I do?"

She didn't have to respond, her face already had. P-Nut may not have hit the nail on the head, but he sure swung the hammer in the right direction.

And, he was right in his initial statement.

Her face and her hair were the same color.

She fanned her face with her hand. "It just got *really* hot in here."

"Give me your panties," P-Nut said flatly.

She gasped. "Pardon..." She cleared her throat. "Pardon me?"

"Your panties," P-Nut whispered. "Give 'em to me."

"I can't--"

"You damned sure can. Reach up in your skirt and peel them off that little wet pussy of yours, and hand em to me."

She sucked a breath. "I'll be...I'd be fired."

"But you want to do it, don't you?"

She swallowed hard, and then nodded lightly.

He tilted his head toward her crotch. "Give 'em to me."

She looked flustered. After shaking her head to clear her thoughts, she looked at me. "Did you say you wanted the ring?"

135

I looked at Nut and let out a sigh of frustration. "I do."

"It's $6,900."

I shrugged. "That's fine."

I handed her the ring and my credit card.

She looked at Nut, held his gaze for a moment, and then walked away ever so gracefully.

I turned toward him and shook my head. "I told you when we came in here to act civil."

"Did not."

"I did too."

"Did not."

"Damn it, Nut I said--"

"You said *act accordingly*," he said. "And, I am. According to the fact she's a sexy red-headed bitch. Red-heads are freaks."

"Where do you come up with this shit? What the fuck, Nut? *Give me your panties*? Jesus H. Christ. You can't tell the Tiffany's clerk to give you her panties."

He crossed his arms and gave me a nod. "Damned sure can. I just did."

P-Nut was an odd individual. Uncommitted and promiscuous as hell, he went from woman to woman, never once settling down. He differed from me in the respect that he'd often have girlfriends, but he could never find anyone courageous enough to stick with him for very long.

His sexual kinks proved to be too much for everyone he'd met to date.

And, he'd *met* many.

Coming from the far side of the store, Jennis sashayed past P-Nut, lightly brushing him as she walked past, and then handed me a bag.

"The receipt's in the bag, and here's your card."

She handed me my credit card and then shook my hand. "It was a pleasure," she said. "I hope that she enjoys the ring for a lifetime."

She turned toward P-Nut and gave a crisp nod. "Thank you, gentlemen, for stopping in."

He returned her nod and turned toward the door.

Without another word, or any additional expressed interest on P-Nut's part, we left. A few feet from the entrance, he glanced over his shoulder.

"Gimme her panties," he said.

"What?"

"Bet she put 'em in the bag."

I glanced at the bag. Stuffed with light blue decorative tissue paper, it was impossible to see what was inside.

I paused, lifted the tissues from the bag, and shook my head. Inside the slightly oversized bag was a small blue box tied with a white silk ribbon. Beside the box, a folded pair of maroon panties with black lace.

"I'll be damned," I said.

"They're in there, ain't they?"

"Here." I handed him the bag. "You can get 'em out."

He pulled out the panties, shoved them in his front pocket, and then reached inside the bag again. He handed me the bag and held up a business card. "And, lookie what we have here. Wrote her phone number on it and everything."

"Fuckin' weirdo," I said.

"Weirdo who's gonna dislocate that skinny bitch's hips."

"Let me know how that high maintenance bitch works out for you, Nut."

He pulled the panties from his front pocket and admired them. "Will

137

do, Smoke."

As we walked toward the parking garage, I expressed my genuine concerns. "Not looking forward to Eddie dating."

He shoved the panties inside his kutte. "Me neither. You doin' the interviews, we doin' em, or you just gonna let me screen the kids and tell you who qualifies?"

I chuckled. "I'll do it."

"Need any help?"

"I sure hope not."

I had no idea how many people were going to want to take Eddie on dates, but I knew one thing: whoever wanted to was going to have to go through me first.

And I wasn't an easy man to impress.

SEVENTEEN

Sandy

I pointed at the corner of the freezer. "Give me two scoops of the cookie dough with a waffle cone, please."

The clerk, who resembled a clean-cut college football player, gave a grin. "Yes ma'am."

I glanced at Craig. "He wants me to meet his daughter. Good idea?"

Without looking up from the various tubs of ice cream in the case, he responded. "Sooner or later, you'll have to."

"Wait!" I shouted as he was taking the second scoop of ice cream. "One cookie dough and one bubble gum."

He looked up. "Are you sure?"

I sighed. "I'm pregnant."

"Are you pregnant and *sure*?"

I shrugged. "For now."

He tossed the scoop aside, got a new one and finished my cone. As he handed it to me, he looked at Craig. "What can I get you?"

"Single scoop, waffle cone, butter pecan, please."

"Oh my God," I said. "I should have got butter pecan."

The clerk looked at me and then at Craig. "She's going to be fun to be around, huh?"

"Oh, it's not mine," Craig said. "We're just friends."

"Oh."

I paid for the ice cream, and we sat down at a high-top table. "I'm nervous."

He took a bite of his ice cream. "About the daughter?"

"Uh huh."

"Just be yourself," he said. "If you're you, she'll love you."

"You think?"

"I *know*."

"I sure hope so."

He took another bite. "So, are you ready for the move in?"

I shrugged. "I think so. I don't know. I mean, not really, but kind of."

"Indecisive much?"

I looked up from my cone. "What do you mean?"

"Yes, no, maybe." He held his cone to the side and shook his head. "Make a decision, Sandy. Life works much better when you commit yourself. When you don't, your heart's not in it. And, when your heart's not in it, you'll fail. Every time."

"Oh. So, if I tell myself I'm ready to do this, it'll work out just fine?" I asked in a sarcastic tone.

"No. You can't just *tell yourself.* You've got to *commit.*"

"How do I do that?"

"Believe? I think that's the first step. Believing it's what you want." He took a bite of his cone and then looked at me. "*I'm moving in with Mr. Biker, and I'm so ready for this. Whatever it takes to make this work, I'm prepared to do. I will not accept failure.* You say that, and you mean it."

"It's that easy?"

He munched about one-third of his cone, and then nodded. "Pretty much."

"I do want it to work, I just have my doubts that it will."

He took a few more bites of the cone and then shook his head. "With an attitude like that, it won't."

"Won't what?"

He poked the end of the cone in his mouth, chewed it, then swallowed. "Work out. If you're sitting here doubting it, you're setting yourself up for a failure. You're destined to fail before you ever start."

Ice cream ran down the cone and onto my hand. I grabbed a napkin and wiped it off. "I'm trying to be realistic."

"Just because every other guy you've been with is a douche, it doesn't mean this guy is." He dabbed the corners of his mouth with a napkin, and then turned to the side. "Good?"

I nodded.

He looked the other direction.

I nodded. "You're good."

"Give him a chance," he said. "Since he asked you to move in, has he done anything stupid?"

"No."

He wadded up the napkin and placed it in the center of the table. "He's probably committed himself to this."

"You think?"

"I hope so."

"But you don't know?"

He let out a sigh. "Assume he has until he does or says something to convince you otherwise. If he is committed, I'm sure you'll see subtle differences in how he acts. Little signs. He may become possessive of you. If he does, it's a good sign."

I nodded slowly as I thought about what he said. "Are you ready?"

"You're not going to eat your cone?" he asked.

I scrunched my nose. "It's gross."

He scooped the trash from the table, stood, and then reached for my cone. "Commit yourself, and assume he's done the same. You'll know pretty soon if he's committed."

"Why do you say that?"

"He's an alpha. Guys like him are possessive. He'll show you in no time if he's committed."

I'd never had a guy be possessive of me, and wondered just how I'd react if Smokey ended up being so. As Craig threw away the cone, I decided I'd just have to wait and see what the future held.

"I hope when he does that I can see it," I said.

"He's a tattooed biker that rides with who? The *Filthy Fuckers*?" He chuckled. "You'll see it."

EIGHTEEN

Smokey

The last few days had been a whirlwind of happenings. With my mind elsewhere, Eddie's birthday crept up on me like a sickness. We had our typical small gathering to celebrate the event, and my stomach was in knots the entire time. As she opened her gifts, my mind filled with visions of installing a revolving door for the boys who were going to come ask permission to take her on out on dates.

Wearing a silver and pink cardboard cone birthday hat he brought himself, P-Nut pushed a neatly-wrapped present across the table. "Do this one first."

She looked at his hat, rolled her eyes, and accepted the gift. After a good shake, she looked at him again. "Why this one?"

"Don't shake the motherfucker, Eddie!" His eyes widened comically as he adjusted his hat. "You'll kill it."

She looked at Nut and cocked her eyebrow. "Do we cuss in the house, P-Nut?"

He lowered his head, feigning shame. "Sorry, Ed. I got excited."

She shook the box lightly. "It's alive?"

His eyebrows slowly raised. "It was when I brought it through the door. Doubt it still is, though. Not after all that. Their little bones are brittle."

She lifted the small box repeatedly, as if trying to guess the weight. "What is it?"

"Reptile," he said flatly.

"It better not be a snake," I said. "I mean it."

There was one thing in earth I feared, and a snake was it. It didn't matter if they were six inches long or six feet long, in my mind they were equally threatening. I'd rather be tortured to death than have a snake within ten feet of me.

The mere thought of coming in contact with one gave me hives.

"You shouldn't be afraid of them," Eddie said. "Snakes are cool. Mr. Freeman has one in class. I get to feed it goldfish."

A shiver ran the length of my spine. The thought of her getting close to a snake made me feel ill.

"Snakes are…" I shook my head. "They're the most vile creatures on earth. If there's one thing that shouldn't exist, a snake is it. I fucking hate 'em."

She looked right at me and raised her eyebrows. "If it's a gift, I have to keep it."

I tilted my head toward the door. "Outside, maybe." I lifted my weight from the seat and nodded toward the box. "Open it."

With me prepared to take off running, she cautiously unwrapped it, revealing a box that had been taped shut with an insane amount of clear packing tape. Several round holes were poked through every side of the box that I could see.

I looked at Nut. His tattoo-covered arms didn't mesh well with his pink birthday hat. I shook my head. "I meant what I said. If that's a snake, you freaking weirdo--"

"I hope it is," Eddie chimed. "*Face your fears*, isn't that what you tell me?" She held out her hand. "Give me your knife, please."

She was right. I did tell her that, and did so often. I handed her my knife. Before I had a chance to speak, she beat me to it.

"Be careful," she said, her voice thick with sarcasm. "It's sharp."

She carefully cut around the top of the box, set the knife aside, and then tilted the top back and peered inside.

"What is it?" I asked.

Her eyes slowly widened.

I pushed myself away from the table. "What is it?"

With reluctance, she reached inside with her index finger and thumb. After what appeared to be a slight struggle, she pulled a snake from the box and flipped it across the table.

I jumped from my seat and screamed. "God damn it!" With a racing heart, I took several quick steps toward the living room and shot P-Nut a glare. "You crazy prick."

While they shared a hearty laugh, I took a glance at the table. The *snake* was sedentary. Sickeningly so.

I studied it.

Rubber.

"It's fake?" I asked hopefully. "Rubber?"

P-Nut struggled to catch his breath. "Yeah." He glanced at Ed, chuckled, and then looked at me. "You don't think I'd bring a real snake in this house, do you?"

My heart was still in my throat. I inhaled a long breath, exhaled, and took another look at the rubber snake. "Hard to say, Nut."

He pointed to the box. "Something else in there. In the bottom."

Eddie peered into the box. She reached in, pulled out a photo, and studied it. "What's this?"

RIGID

"What the fu--" He cocked an eyebrow and nodded toward what she held. "What's it look like?"

"Volkswagen."

"Beetle," P-Nut said. "Or Bug. They call 'em both."

She wrinkled her nose. "What's it for?"

"Pin it up on your wall." He shrugged. "Or take it to school and show your friends, hell, I don't know."

I reached for the picture. "What is it? A picture of a Volkswagen?"

She handed me the picture. It was a photo of an old-school Volkswagen Beetle in remarkable condition. The picture was taken beside his beloved Old-School Harley, obviously taken in P-Nut's driveway.

I wrinkled my nose and looked at Nut.

"Engine's locked up, but other than that, it's perfect. Old lady in Encinitas had it. Took me four hours and half a pot of coffee talk her into selling it. Figured by the time you were old enough to drive it, you and your dad could pull the motor and rebuild it. Fits your personality."

She gasped. "It's mine? Like, that's *my* car?"

P-Nut nodded.

She jumped from her chair and opened her arms. "I love you, P-Nut. Thank you."

He stood and gave her a hug. "Love you too, Ed."

I shook my head and swallowed pridefully. P-Nut was a great friend to me, and somewhat of an uncle to Eddie, but he was also her friend.

I crossed my arms in front of my chest. "You bought her a car?"

He nodded. "Volkswagen."

"I saw the picture," I said. "She can't drive for another year."

He shrugged. "We can get it towed over here, and you'll have a year to get the motor fixed." He motioned toward the box. "There's a *Best*

Buy gift card in there, too. Go pick out a stereo for it. Got to have tunes if you're going to roll in style."

Eddie hugged P-Nut again. "Thank you, thank you, thank you."

"Did you wear that little hat?" I asked.

"What?"

"When you went to talk to the old lady. Did you wear that goofy little hat?"

He reached for the hat. "No, I got this fucker at the Wal Mart on my way here. You know, that place is full of a bunch of fucking weirdos, but when a 1%er walks in, he gets all the stares."

"They're not staring at you as a 1%er, Nut. They're staring at you because you're weird."

"Nobody can tell if I'm weird or normal by lookin' at me."

"You've got a tattoo of Goofy on one arm, and Mickey Mouse on the other. It's pretty clear."

He looked at his forearm. "It's Pluto. Pluto. Pluto. How many times I told you that?"

"Pluto. Goofy. What's the difference?"

"Pluto's a dog with a collar. Goofy wears boots and clothes and shit. Big difference."

"I'll try and remember that," I said. "And, thanks, Brother."

He gave me a nod and then shot Eddie a smile. "She only turns seventeen once."

After the excitement of the car faded, Eddie opened several gifts that P-Nut and I had bought her, none of which were earth-shattering. After everything had been opened, I reached into my kutte, and pulled out the last one.

"Oh, wait. There's one more."

"There's more?"

I handed her the small box. "Here."

She looked at the blue box, and then straightened the silk ribbon. "What is it?"

"One way to find out."

She carefully removed the bow, and then stared at the Tiffany & Co insignia for a moment. After looking at me, and then P-Nut, she removed the top and peered inside.

Her eyebrows raised. "Oh. My. God."

She glanced at me, and reached inside the box. "Is it real?"

"Sure is."

She lifted the ring from the box. "What…why…oh wow. But. What…"

"I figured if you were going to start dating, you should be wearing a ring that made you look like you were spoken for. It'll scare off the meek, and save both of us a lot of grief."

"Holy crap. It's awesome."

"Put it on."

She put the ring on her wedding finger, and then let her hand dangle over the table. The ring did nothing but accentuate her beauty.

"I love it," she said.

"Looks good as fuck," P-Nut said. "Classy."

She shot him a scornful look.

He shrugged. "Just slipped out. Sorry."

She came around the edge of the table and gave me a hug. "Dad, you're the best."

I held her in my arms for some time, clinging to that moment. All I could do was hope that she felt the same way after I broke the news to her about Sandy.

Because having her views of me change would certainly crush me.

NINETEEN

Sandy

Nervous wouldn't come close to describing how I felt. After a long discussion, Smokey decided I should meet Eddie at dinner before he broke the news to her about everything. I couldn't say that I disagreed with his logic, but my stomach sure seemed to.

My current state of being was *emotional*. Period. Everything, as far as I was concerned, was a disaster. Hoping that the night unfolded without me bursting into tears for no reason, I pulled into the driveway and shut off the engine.

Their home, a small ranch, was in one of the nicer areas in town. From the outside, it was apparent that Smokey took meticulous care of it. Every tree, plant, and shrub was perfectly groomed, and although most of the homes didn't have grass lawns, his did, and it was a luscious green color.

I took a deep breath, opened the car door, and stepped into the driveway.

The front door opened.

I met Smokey's gaze and couldn't help but smile. He was dressed in jeans, boots, and a stark white tee-shirt, but no kutte.

"I'm coming," I said.

He stepped onto the porch and grinned. "You look fantastic."

"Thank you."

I'd carefully chosen a dress that was conservative, but not too much so. A floral fabric that was form-fitting, it was the best of both worlds.

I stepped onto the porch. "Is this dress okay? Is it too tight?"

He opened his arms and gave me a hug. As he released me, he leaned back and looked me over. "It's perfect. You look like a model."

I brushed my hands along my hips. "Thank you."

Me reached for the bag I was carrying. "You brought wine?"

"Sparkling grape juice."

He grinned. "She'll like that. C'mon."

I followed him into the house. A faint hint of garlic filled the air, and alluded to what we'd be eating for dinner. As soon as I entered, I greedily scanned what would soon be my new home.

The open floor plan made the home seem larger than it was, but it wasn't small by any means. The living room was tastefully decorated, and without an ounce of clutter. A wall separated the kitchen from the living room, but I could see into the kitchen.

Standing in front of the counter, preoccupied with the contents of a large bowl, stood a gorgeous woman who was tall and thin with light brown hair. Dressed in jeans, Chucks, and a tight-fitting tee-shirt, she was breathtaking.

"Is that Eddie?" I whispered.

"The one and only."

"She's gorgeous."

His eyes lit up. "Thank you."

I instantly filled with excitement about getting to know her better, and befriending her over time. As she carefully placed objects in the bowl, Smokey took me by the hand and led me into the kitchen.

"Eddie," he said. "This is Sandy."

As soon as he said *Eddie*, she turned around. When she noticed me, she smiled, and it was easy for me to see that it was genuine.

I had no idea what to expect from her, and figured it would either go one of two ways. Complete and instantaneous rejection, or excitement.

She would either be pleased that her father had finally found someone worthy of his – and her – attention, or she would feel threatened by his new relationship, and me. Seeing her face led me to believe it was the former.

She wiped her hands on a towel, and then extended her right hand. "It's a pleasure to meet you." She looked me up and down. "Your dress is uhhm. It's beautiful."

"It's a pleasure to meet *you*," I said. "Thank you. Can I do anything to help?"

She shook her head. "I'm done. Basically."

She looked at her dad, smiled, and then held his gaze for a moment. "If you want, you could help me get everything set on the table."

"Sure." I looked at Smokey, then turned toward her and smiled. "I'd love to."

Smokey set my bag on the counter. "I'm going to go wash up."

Oh God.

Don't leave us alone.

"He likes everything perfect," she whispered, "See this salad?"

I peered into the bowl she'd been working on when we walked in. Tomato wedges were perfectly placed on top of the various leaves of lettuce around the circumference of the bowl.

"Uh huh."

"If that was all mixed up, he'd throw a fit."

I looked at her in disbelief. I would have never guessed that about him. "Really?"

"True story," she said. "And see this?" She pointed to two casserole dishes that were filled with stuffed pasta. "One's Manicotti," she said. "And the other is cannelloni. According to him, they can't be in the same dish. He says they're different pastas, so they can't touch each other. And, he says they taste *different*. He likes them both."

"Oh. Wow."

She glanced over her shoulder and then looked at me. "He's a weirdo. I'm sure he didn't tell you that, though."

I grinned. "He didn't, no."

"So, on the table, he likes the main course in the center, and the salad and bread on the outside."

"Okay."

Using oven mitts, she carried one of the casserole dishes to the table and set it on a stone trivet. "Just like that."

"Hear the music?" she asked.

I hadn't noticed it until she said something, but after she mentioned it, I noticed the faint sound of music came from the living room. What was playing sounded like an old-school ballad.

I nodded. "Yeah."

"It plays all day. All night. Even when the T.V. is on. That's another thing." She smiled. "Like I said. He's different."

She placed the other casserole dish on the table, and then looked at me. "I *really* like that dress. I need to wear them more often. Where'd you get it?"

"The T.J. Maxx, out by Vista."

She shrugged. "Never been there."

"I like bargains. I shop there all the time. They've got good stuff, and it's cheap."

She looked me over again. "It's really pretty."

I nodded toward her feet. "I like your shoes, and I'm not just saying that. I really like them. I wear Chucks all the time."

She nodded toward my 2" heels. "I'd wear 'em with that dress."

I glanced toward the living room, and then looked at her. "I should have," I whispered.

"Want to see something cool?" She asked.

"Sure."

She pointed toward the table. "Bread and the salad go on the outside, by his chair. I'll be right back."

I glanced at the table. All the chairs looked the same. "Which one's his?"

"The one that points toward the door," she said over her shoulder. "Be right back."

She sprinted out of the kitchen. Nervously, I placed the salad and the basket of bread on the table, situating them an even distance from one another. Before I made myself comfortable with their placement, she came rushing to my side.

She handed me a small printed photo. "Look at *that*."

I looked at the picture. A brick-red Volkswagen sitting beside a Harley-Davidson in someone's driveway was all there was to see.

I had no idea if I was supposed to be looking at the Harley or the car. "Oh wow," I said.

"It's mine."

I still had no idea. I knew it was her birthday a few days prior, but hadn't heard what she'd received. I didn't suspect Smokey would buy her a Harley, so I rolled the dice and guessed the car was hers.

"That car?" I asked excitedly. "It's *yours*?"

"P-Nut gave it to me." She nodded eagerly. "Have you met him yet?"

"I haven't."

"He's really sweet."

"I like it. A lot. Guess what?"

She reached for the photo. "What?"

I walked to the sink and lifted the blinds. "Look in the driveway."

My Volkswagen, although newer that hers, was a Beetle as well. It wasn't much, but it might be enough that we could somehow develop a bond over our cars, if nothing else.

She peered over my shoulder. "Is that yours?"

"Yep."

"I like it. Yellow's a cool color."

"It's got a little flower vase on the dash, and I keep real flowers in it," I said. "Well, most of the time. Sometimes they're pretty wilted."

She smiled. "That's awesome."

"Happy late birthday, by the way."

"Thank you."

I turned around, reached for my bag, and pulled out a small wrapped box. "I got this for you. Sorry it's late."

"You didn't have to--"

"I know." I shrugged one shoulder dismissively. "It's just something small."

She unwrapped it, opened the box and smiled. "Oh my God. I love it."

"Some of the proceeds went to the *Let Girls Learn* fund, and the bracelet is called *Girl Power*, so I thought it was fitting."

The bracelet, an Alex and Ani gold bangle bracelet, had a daisy charm, a *because I'm a girl* charm, a heart, and a Peace Corps charm.

"Are you serious?" she asked.

"About what?"

"It's called *girl power*?"

I nodded. "That's what it's called."

She raised her hand high in the air. "Girl Power."

I slapped my hand against hers.

"Girl power is my mantra," she said. "This is awesome."

She slipped it over her wrist, and I noticed she already wore a similar bracelet. I grinned at the thought of her actually liking what I had given her.

After she got it situated, she opened her arms. "Thank you."

As she hugged me I decided she was an awesome person, and that although we weren't too far apart in age, she'd be an equally awesome step-daughter if the day ever came that Smokey and I were officially together.

As we finished setting the table, I realized that she'd also be a big sister to the life that was slowly growing inside of me.

I took a quick look at her. She was absolutely adorable, and reminded me more of a mother or a wife than a daughter who was still in high school. The thought of her being a sister to our baby made me happy.

Really happy.

"Smells good," Smokey said.

The sound of his voice caused me to turn around. When I saw him, I sucked in an unexpected breath.

He was dressed in a plaid long-sleeved pearl snap shirt like the surfers often wore. Neatly pressed, and untucked, it was in complete contrast to what he normally wore.

Seeing him wearing it caused me to smile.

I looked him up and down. His jeans were new, too. "You look nice," I said.

His blue eyes glistened. "Thanks."

"Did you wash your hands?" Eddie asked.

He held them up. "Yep."

"I need to wash mine," I said.

"Bathroom's that way." Eddie pointed toward the living room. "We'll eat when you get back."

I turned toward the doorway that led to the living room. Smokey stood in the threshold of the door. When I attempted to walk past him, he stopped me. Then, something unexpected happened.

Very unexpected.

With his index finger, he lifted my chin ever so slightly, gazing down at me as he did so. Our eyes locked, and he leaned toward me.

My heart skipped a beat.

I thought for an instant that he was going to kiss me, but he paused. With his lips only an inch from mine, he hovered over me and gazed into my eyes. At that instant, after being duped into thinking a kiss was imminent, I forgot how to breathe. My heart pounded into my ribs, reassuring me with each beat how much I wanted him to do so.

I sucked in a quick breath and stood on quivering legs, wishing he would have.

And then, he did.

Our mouths met and melted into one another. My eyes fell closed.

The kiss was soft, and subtle, but far more powerful than any kiss I'd ever experienced.

Our lips parted, and I opened my eyes.

He released my chin and grinned. "First door on the right."

While I washed my hands, I realized it was the first time we'd kissed. I remembered what Craig had told me about Smokey taking possession of me, and decided that the kiss was the first step. Feeling giddy, I returned to the kitchen and sat in front of the only available place setting.

Smokey looked at Eddie. "You or me?"

"My turn." She bowed her head.

Smokey looked at me, clasped his hands together, and then lowered his head.

I did the same.

"Heavenly Father. We thank you for our health, for this food we are so fortunate to have before us, and for the addition of Dad's friend, Sandy to our table. I ask that you look over P-Nut, and take a special look at Ramone Sanchez, as he wrecked his bicycle yesterday, and broke his leg. Please bless this food, Lord, so it may make us stronger, and with that strength, make us more able to serve you. As always, in your name, Amen."

Smokey lifted his head and looked at Eddie. "Pass me the cannelloni, please."

She picked up the dish and shot him a glare. "Guests first."

That evening at dinner, I realized that falling in love with Smokey wasn't going to be difficult at all.

Because it was already happening.

TWENTY

Smokey

I'd postponed the inevitable for as long as I could, and it was time for me to come clean with Eddie. I wasn't sure what would be more difficult for her to accept; the news of the pregnancy, or that Sandy was going to move in.

I guessed in a matter of minutes, I'd know the answer. I peeked into her bedroom. "You got a minute, Ed?"

In the middle of hanging up laundry, she looked up. "What's up?"

"When you get done."

"When I get done what?"

"When you get done, do you have a minute?"

"I've got a minute, now. What's up?"

"I'll wait 'till you're done."

"Then you should have stuck your head in my door and said, *hey Ed, I'm too busy to talk now, but I'll have a minute when you're done, wanna talk later?*"

"Sometimes it's hard for me to believe you're my child."

She threaded the hanger she held through the neck of a shirt, and then glared at me. "I'm a seventeen-year-old female version of you."

"I don't know about that."

"It's true," she said. "You're a smart ass, I'm a smart ass. You like music, I like music. You're a badass, I'm a badass--"

"Watch your mouth," I said.

She rolled her eyes. "You cuss all the time, and I get in trouble for saying *anything*. Maybe we're not so much alike. No, wait. We *are* alike, we just play by different rules. Yeah, that's it."

"When you're eighteen, you can cuss all you want."

"Yeah," she said. "*Outside*."

I laughed. "That's your rule, not mine."

She hung up her last shirt. "It's a good rule. If I let you and P-Nut cuss as much as you wanted, I'd be tripping over cusswords all the time. You two are awful."

"We're bikers. What do you expect?"

She closed her closet door and then looked at me and shrugged. "Manners?"

"I slip up from time to time."

"You didn't slip up once when Sandy was here. Did you notice that?"

"I didn't notice."

Her eyebrows raised and her head tilted to the side. "I did."

I saw it as an opportunity to start the discussion I'd been dreading. "Maybe she brings out the good in me."

"Maybe she does." She brushed the wrinkles from her comforter, and then looked up. "Can I ask you a question?"

"Sure."

"There's never been a woman in this house. Not one. Ever. Why?"

I wanted to tell her it was out of respect, but feared ten minutes later that she'd crucify me for saying it. I chewed on my response for a minute, and realized there was nothing I could do to make it taste good.

"I didn't want to hurt you."

She sat on the edge of her bed. "How would having a woman in this home hurt me?"

I sat down on the bed beside her and rested my forearms on my knees. "I always figured if I introduced you to a woman, and you liked her enough to let her into your heart, that if she up and left one day." I shook my head at the thought of it and then looked up. "I knew it would hurt you."

"It'd hurt you, too. Right?"

I nodded. "I suppose so, why?"

"You wouldn't bring some random girl home that you didn't like. If you brought her here and introduced me to her, it'd mean you liked her a lot, right?"

"Yeah."

"If you brought her here based on your best judgement, and then things went to crap, it wouldn't be because you did anything wrong. It'd just mean she wasn't able to see what an awesome guy you are. So, we'd both be hurt, but you more than me."

"Why's that?"

"Because you'd see me hurt, and that would hurt you. And then you'd hurt from what she did to you." She looked at me and shrugged. "Double whammy."

"The double whammy." I chuckled, and then gazed down at the floor and nodded my head. One thing I always admired about Eddie as her intellect, and she was reminding me why.

"I'm not letting anyone into my heart until I'm sure about them," she said. "So, I really don't have to worry about being hurt like you do."

I sat and stared at the floor, trying to find the words to continue.

After a few seconds, she broke the silence. "Are you okay?"

163

I realized I was still nodding my head. I stopped, and then looked up "I'm good."

"Something's on your mind."

There was only one way to get through it, and that was to do it. I inhaled a breath, let half of it out, and began.

"Did you like Sandy?"

"Yeah. A lot. She's cool, and she's pretty as eff."

"Pretty as eff?"

She looked embarrassed. "Pretty as F, U, C, K."

"Oh." I gazed down at the floor and nodded. "Yeah, she's awfully pretty, that's for sure."

"Why?" she asked.

I let out a long sigh.

She leaned over and kissed my cheek. "If you like her enough to make her the first girl you've ever introduced to me, I'd like her just because *you* liked her that much. If she's that important to you, she's important to me, too."

I nodded, and then looked at her. "Thanks, Ed."

"But I like her anyway. She's cool."

"Cool?"

"Yeah. Uhhm. Did you see that dress, mister?" she asked excitedly. "And she drives a Bug. Did P-Nut know that?"

"I don't think so."

"Does he know her?"

I didn't want to tell her how, and hoped she didn't ask. "Yeah."

"How'd you meet?"

"We met at the Crab Shack on Harbor Drive. Cholo and Lex introduced me to her. She works with Lex."

"Have you been seeing her for a while?"

I started the nodding again. "Yeah."

"Well, I like her. A lot."

The last thing in the world I wanted to do was hurt her, but I was beginning to look at the direction of the conversation we were having as playful and inaccurate. I needed to say what it was I came to, but doing it wasn't as easy as I had hoped.

I sat up, looked right at her, and sighed. "I want her to move in with us. What would you think about that?"

Her eyes went wide, but not drastically. She seemed far more excited than anything. Seeing her excitement was reassuring.

"Really?"

I couldn't recall the last time I had cried. If I had to guess, I would say it was the day Ed was born, and although it may have qualified as crying, it was more like a leaky eye. Tears simply ran down my face when I saw her.

But. For whatever reason, I was on the cusp of breaking down in tears. With swollen eyes, I looked at her and nodded.

"Yeah."

She scooted in a circle until she was facing me, and then pulled her legs onto the bed and sat beside me cross-legged. "Uhhm. Like permanently? Like you and her would be together? I mean, you'd be officially *together*?"

My mouth had gone dry, and responding verbally wasn't an option. As I fought back the tears, I pressed my tongue to the roof of my mouth and nodded.

She rested her hand on my thigh and smiled. "I think I'd like that."

I couldn't continue beating around the bush. I needed to simply tell

RIGID

Eddie the truth. Anything short of that was a lie.

I was many things, but a liar wasn't one of them.

I'd raised Eddie the way I was raised. There were two things on earth: right, and wrong. Two colors, black and white. My world had zero shades of gray. Things were either on the left side of the line or on the right.

In my world, there was nothing that needed pondered. I realized not everyone would agree with my perceptions, but everything fell into one or the other of those two categories.

My beliefs, or so I hoped, were shared by Eddie. If that were the case, she'd be able to understand the position I was in.

I looked right at her, and then wiped my eyes with the heel of my palms.

Her face washed with concern. "What's wrong?"

"Gimme a second." I held up my index finger, drew a choppy breath, and then continued. "Sandy and I…we uhhm. We met, and we went out. We liked each other, a lot. We uhhm. We went on a few dates, and we had…we had sex. And, she uhhm…"

My voice was shaky, and each word seemed to be getting stuck in the back of my dry throat. While I struggled to continue, she swallowed heavily, and then met my gaze.

"Is she pregnant?"

I bit into my lower lip and nodded my head lightly. "Yeah. She is."

Her eyes dropped. I had no idea what she was thinking, but I knew hurting her would simply kill me. As much as I realized I had to do the right thing by Sandy, I further knew I couldn't do anything to sacrifice my relationship with Eddie.

As she seemed to be digesting everything, emotion washed over me, leaving me feeling vulnerable and weak.

"There's only one thing you can do." She looked up. "The *right* thing."

Everything was still tangled up in my throat, but I opened my arms and managed to rid myself of three words.

"I love you."

She hugged me. "I love you, too."

Sitting on the edge of her bed, we held each other. I cried a little bit, but they weren't tears of sadness. In realizing the level of maturity and understanding in the seventeen-year-old girl I had raised since birth, I filled with so much pride it seemed to force the tears from my eyes.

We sat there in each other's arms for a long while, and then she broke our embrace. When she realized I was crying, she reached up and wiped the tears from my cheeks with her thumbs.

"Be careful what you wish for," she said. "Remember that?"

Embarrassed, I wiped my eyes with my index fingers. "What about it?"

"You've always told me that," she said. "And guess what?"

"What?"

She shrugged one shoulder. "I've always wanted a sister."

TWENTY ONE

Sandy

I'd always performed in an altered state of being. When I got on stage, I never did so as Sandy, I was always Texxxas. And, when I went home, Texxxas remained in the dressing room, where she belonged.

It left Sandy immune to everything that happened in the club, and allowed her to live a life unaffected by the men who lusted over Texxxas.

The process had worked well for me.

Until now.

It seemed that lately Texxxas was spending all her time on stage thinking about Smokey. My two worlds were somehow colliding, and I didn't like the result.

"Fuck yeah," someone screamed. "Look at her big fucking titties. I'd like to stick my cock between 'em and…"

"Skinny little bitch needs fucked," another hollered.

"Show us your tits!"

"Yeah, show us your tits!"

I turned slowly, gyrating my hips to the beat of the music, wishing all along that I hadn't given any notice. I regretted not walking in and simply quitting. For the first time since I started dancing, I felt guilty for doing so. It wasn't because I perceived the profession as *wrong*, because I didn't.

But I could no longer separate the real me from the make believe me, and the girl who was on stage was slowly falling for a man who asked her to stop performing.

And I hadn't.

As I turned toward the front of the stage, I heard shouting from the entrance of the club. It grew louder and louder, and then I saw Craig rush in the direction of the commotion. I tried to focus on the music, lose touch with whatever might be happening, and simply make it to the end of the song without becoming an emotional mess.

"Show us your pussy," someone hissed.

"Fuck yeah! Take that fucking bikini off!"

One of the men who was shouting got up and began to climb on the edge of the elevated platform where I was dancing. I glanced at where Craig normally stood, only to realize he hadn't returned.

The overeager patron pulled himself onto the side of the dance floor, rose to his feet, and began writhing to the music as he shuffled toward me.

"You're a sexy little bitch," he said, his tongue thick from the alcohol he'd consumed. "Come here. I'll help you get that top off."

Still dressed in my bikini, I folded my arms over my chest in protest of his offer. "Get off the stage!" I said through my teeth.

"Hey motherfucker," a familiar voice shouted. "Get the fuck away from her!"

I looked up.

Oh shit.

Smokey and another man were mere feet from the front of the platform and coming in my direction as fast as they could maneuver around the tables.

The music stopped.

Short of the commotion in front of me, the club fell silent.

"What the fuck?" someone shouted.

A group of men stood from their table and turned toward Smokey and his friend.

"What the fuck, dude?" one of them said. "She was getting' ready to show us her puss."

While his friend continued toward the stage, Smokey spun to face the three men and began a very one-sided fight.

In my time at the club, I'd seen many fights, several of which involved bikers, but I'd never seen three guys get their asses kicked *that* quickly. In three or four punches, and what appeared to be one headbutt, the three men were on the floor at Smokey's feet.

I glanced to my left.

Smokey's friend, who I now recognized as a club regular named P-Nut, had climbed onto the platform. Upon seeing him, the man who was approaching me pulled a knife from his pocket and flicked it open with a *click!*

Oh shit.

"He's got a knife!" I shouted.

P-Nut glanced at the knife, and then looked at the man and grinned. I couldn't believe my eyes.

Why are you smiling?

"Better bring more than that if you wanna fuck with the Nut," he said, laughing as he spoke.

The knife-wielding man took a quick step toward him.

P-Nut extended his arms and curled his fingertips toward his palms as if inviting the man to come closer. "C'mon, motherfucker. Come cut the Nut."

With my mouth agape, I stared in disbelief.

What's wrong with you?

He's got a knife.

The man lunged forward and swung the knife wildly toward P-Nut's chest.

P-Nut blocked the swing, gripped the man's wrist, and then extended his arm straight. While the man's eyes widened, P-Nut thrust his open hand against the man's elbow, breaking his arm with a loud *crack*!

The man screamed in pain and the knife fell to the floor.

A few quick fists to the man's midsection followed, and then he fell to the floor in a pile. Clutching an arm that now dangled at an awful angle, the man began to blubber.

"You broke…my fucking…you broke my arm!"

P-Nut shrugged and reached for the knife laying at his feet. "Shoulda listened, dumbass."

He picked up the knife, put it in his pocket, and then looked at me. "Name's P-Nut." He reached for my hand. "C'mon. I'll help you down."

Still in shock from what I'd seen, I accepted his offer and then glanced toward where Smokey had been standing. Just a few feet from the edge of the platform, and now in an all-out bar room brawl, Smokey was swinging his fists toward anyone who got near him. Most men were running toward the door, but everyone within arm's reach was being pummeled.

Out of the corner of my eye, I saw Craig rushing toward him.

"Hey, you Dwayne Johnson looking motherfucker!" P-Nut shouted from beside me. "Stay away from him!"

Craig looked up, and his eyes immediately shot wide. After coming to a complete stop, his hands slowly raised above his shoulders.

I glanced to my left.

P-Nut held a gun in his hand, and it was pointing right at Craig.

Oh, God.

Please don't...

"Stay the fuck away from him," P-Nut said, waving the pistol to the side. "Just step to the side, and everything's gonna be cool. We're just takin' her home, and those fellas was bein' disrespectful to her."

Craig stood, frozen in place, with his hands raised to shoulder height.

The man on the platform floor continued to cry out in pain, and there were no less than six men on the floor below us doing the same. After walking me to the edge of the platform, P-Nut shouted at Smokey.

"Smoke!" he yelled. "Time to roll."

Smokey, holding a rather limp man up by his shirt, pounded him once more in the face with his right hand. After dropping him to the floor, he turned toward me.

"You're done working here." His voice was stern. "It's over."

The thought of having him lose trust in me was crushing. I leaned over the edge of the stage. "I gave notice, I was just--"

His eyes narrowed and his forehead creased. "O-ver."

I swallowed heavily. My guess was that he just took possession of me, and as weird as it seemed, I loved it.

I fell into his arms as if I didn't have a care in the world. As he caught me, I looked up. "Okay."

He lowered me to the floor, scanned the club, and upon seeing no threats, pulled off his kutte. He handed it to P-Nut and then took off his wife beater.

"Put this on," he said.

RIGID

"Go ahead, Smoke," P-Nut said. "I got your back."

Smokey looked at me with angry eyes. "Stay between us," he demanded.

I pulled his shirt over my head. "Okay."

With Smokey leading the way, the three of us walked past the overturned tables and toward the door. When we reached the entrance, the two doormen, who were also bouncers, were standing there.

"Step aside fellas," Smokey said dryly.

"Let 'em through," I heard Craig say from behind me.

They stepped to the side of the door.

"Smokey, wait," I said. "I want you to meet someone."

He spun around and shot me a hard look. "What?"

"I want you to meet someone," I said sheepishly.

Obviously still on an adrenaline rush from the fights he'd been in, he glared at me as if I had asked him to jump off the San Francisco Bridge. I tilted my head to the side. "This is Craig. He's my best friend."

Craig cleared his throat. "Her *gay* best friend."

Smokey gave the two doormen and angry glare, glanced at Craig, and lifted his chin ever so slightly. "Nice to meet you."

I shrugged and then put on an awkward smile. "This is my baby's daddy."

"I'm not your *baby daddy*," Smokey growled. "I'm your Ol' Man."

With my eyes still fixed on Craig, my mouth curled into a prideful grin. "Didn't take long, did it?"

He gave me the *thumbs up*.

"Mail my check?"

Craig simply smiled.

"What was that about?" Smokey asked.

"Inside joke," I said.

That night I walked out the door of the club for the last time, with my Ol' Man leading the way, and P-Nut watching our backs.

And, it felt *right*.

TWENTY TWO

Smokey

It seemed odd mentoring a prospect when I normally didn't allow anyone close to me other than the small group of people I trusted. Trusting Tank was different than mentoring him, but he was slowly making strides toward gaining my trust, nonetheless.

"I'll do whatever it takes to get in this club, believe me," he said. "I had that feeling of brotherhood in the Corps, and after they wouldn't up my tour, I lost it. I miss it, and the only place I think I can get it is in an MC."

I took a bite of my burger. "Why wouldn't they up your tour?"

"PTSD. Said I was a threat to my fellow Marines."

"Damned shame," I said. "Couple of the patches are vets, and they've got PTSD, too. Sucks."

He shoved a handful of French fries in his mouth and nodded. "I deal with it different than most, I suppose."

"What do you do to deal with it?"

He grabbed another handful of fries. "Go to the range."

"I shot him a surprised look. "That's it?"

"Flying bullets make me happy."

I couldn't decide if his response made me nervous or not. "Suppose it depends on which direction they're going."

His eyes narrowed slightly. "What do you mean?"

"Whether they're coming at you, or going away from you."

"Shit," he said. "I'll take 'em either way."

"I prefer the ones that aren't flying in my direction."

"Either way's exciting." He nodded toward my pistol. "See you carry a piece. Gives me peace of mind knowing that."

"Gives me peace of mind, too." I slapped my hand against my pocket. "Just like the American Express Card. *Don't leave home without it.*"

"I'm with ya on that."

Tank was in his late twenties by my guess, and had spent ten years in the military, all of which was in combat. He was average height, and way above average size, hence the name *Tank*. His head – still sporting a military crew cut – seemed to sit on top of his muscular shoulders, and he didn't have the "V" shape that most men sought. He was simply *big*. And muscular.

One of his massive biceps was adorned with the Eagle, Globe, and Anchor, and the other was tattooed with what I suspected was his unit number, and several names.

I assumed the names were of Marines lost in combat, but didn't ask.

"Soon as you're done finger fucking those fries, we'll go check on that job," I said. "See if my guy's done with it or not."

"How many jobs you do at once?" he asked.

"Depends. Sometimes one, sometimes five or six. Right now, Cholo's keeping me pretty busy with a few, and I've got a couple others that I'm doing. Need as many as I can, though. Got a kid on the way and all."

"That chick move in yet?"

"Nope. We're moving her this weekend."

"Need any help?"

"We got it covered."

"I'm serious." He flexed his bicep. "I love liftin' heavy shit."

"I'll keep that in mind."

I'd always said you could tell who your real friends were by who showed up on moving day, and the fact he offered made me feel good about him being a solid dude.

He grabbed another fistful of fries, and bit the tips off half of them in one bite. "If you decide you need some help, I'm serious. Just give me a holler."

"Will do."

"My Ol' Lady left me when I was in Afghanistan. I don't know, when I see a fucker like you settling down with some chick, it gives me hope."

"Fucker like me." I chuckled. "What the fuck's that mean, *prospect*?"

"No disrespect, but you're a fucking asshole," he said.

I laughed. "No argument from me on that."

As he finished devouring his fries, I considered what he'd said about being ditched by his Ol' Lady while he was at war. I normally didn't feel sorry for anyone, but I began to feel sorry for him to go through such a loss while he was fighting for his country's freedom.

"Suck's about your Ol' lady," I said. "Leaving like that."

"Standard Operating Procedure for wives of Marines," he said. "Seems they all do it, eventually."

I shook my head. "Damned shame."

"I want a woman who I can trust. Tough, considering I don't trust anyone."

"You trust me?" I cocked an eyebrow, and waited for his response.

He finished his handful of fries and then shook his head. "Nope. Haven't given me a reason to yet. If you want to gain my trust, you'll have to earn it. Suppose the same goes for you, right?"

I pursed my lips and nodded. He was slowly earning my respect. In time, I was sure trust would follow.

"C'mon," I said. "Let's beat feet."

"Sorry, Boss. I got to hit the head and drop a deuce. Be back post haste. Those greasy fries are goin' right through me."

"I don't need all the gory details about you taking a shit, *prospect*. Hurry the fuck up."

While he was taking a dump, I sent Sandy a text message and asked how her day was going. It seemed strange caring about someone other than Eddie, P-Nut or myself, but it wasn't something I had to tell myself to do, which led me to believe I naturally cared about her, the baby, or both.

She responded with an emoji of some sort that I wasn't able to discern, as her iPhone and my Android didn't communicate well with each other when it came to smiley faces and other like-minded shit.

I grinned, pocketed my phone, and checked my watch. We'd been in the restaurant for almost an hour, which was a long time for me to sit in one place during the day. When I was about to get up and leave, Tank came out of the bathroom.

"Take my advice, you'll wanna use the women's restroom if you gotta go."

I stood and shook my head. "I'm good. Let's roll."

We walked outside, and no more than reached the parking lot, when Tank spotted someone leaning over my bike. Before I had a chance to say anything, he took off in a dead run toward the guy.

"Hey, motherfucker, what are you doing?" he shouted.

The guy, who was leaned over the gas tank, stood and turned to face him. His face did little to hide the fact he'd been caught fucking with something he knew he surely shouldn't have been.

Knowing that the man hadn't done any damage, I paused to see just how Tank would handle the situation.

"I was just--" the man stammered.

Tank stepped in front of him, partially blocking my view. "Just what?"

"I was, uhh--"

Tank punched him in the gut, then kicked his legs out from underneath him. The man fell to the asphalt at Tank's feet.

"When a motherfucker takes too long to answer," Tank said as he kicked the man. "That's when you can tell a lie's coming."

He kicked the guy in the gut a few more times, and he immediately covered his head with his arms, hoping to protect his face from any boot damage.

Tank shoved his heel against the man's hip, rolled him onto his back, and then pressed his boot to the man's throat.

"Don't ever fuck with a man's bike. Don't look at it, breathe on it, take pictures of it, and you damned sure better not touch it."

"O-okay."

Tank lifted his foot. "Get the fuck outta here."

The man rose to his feet, looked at me, and then turned and ran behind the adjoining restaurant.

Tank turned toward me. "Fucking shit head."

I chuckled and then shook my head. "Fifteen years of riding, and that's the first time anyone's ever got near my shit."

"Burns my ass when a man fucks with my sled."

"Apparently."

"Sorry I jumped him. Shoulda let you handle it, but that's just how I roll."

I slapped him on the back. "You did good, *prospect*."

He didn't know it, but he just earned a few points toward gaining my trust, and a few at earning a little more respect.

Hell, at the rate he was going, he'd be running with P-Nut and me in a few years.

"I'll take that help moving Sandy if it still stands," I said.

He turned toward me and nodded once. "Might keep me out of trouble."

"Plan on it, then."

I always wanted a little brother to harass, and realized Tank just might be able to fill those shoes.

With Sandy moving in, the pregnancy going without a hitch, Eddie healthy and happy, and Tank to harass, my life was looking up.

Or, so I thought.

TWENTY THREE

Sandy

Cholo, Lex, and Tank had just left, leaving P-Nut, Eddie, Smokey and me at standing in the living room looking at a stack or cardboard boxes. I'd minimized my belongings to personal effects and a few pieces of furniture that Smokey and I agreed would be well-suited for his home.

Correction.

Our home.

"Relax." Smokey waved his arm toward the couch. "Nut and I will get those boxes taken to the bedroom."

"I can get them, they're mine. And, they're not heavy."

"Gotta respect a bitch that'll carry her own boxes," P-Nut said.

Bitch?

"She ain't picking up shit, she's pregnant. "Smokey glared at him. "An, you need to watch it, Nut."

"Watch what? The compliments?"

"Calling her a bitch."

Thank you.

P-Nut shrugged one shoulder. "Didn't call her a bitch."

"You said, *gotta respect a bitch that'll carry her own boxes.*"

"Yep, sure did."

"And, I'm saying you need to watch it."

"Big difference between saying what I said and calling someone a bitch."

Eager to hear his explanation, my head swiveled back and forth between P-Nut and Smokey.

Smokey put his hands on his hips and sighed. "You just called her a bitch."

"Listen carefully," P-Nut said. "*Gotta respect a bitch that'll carry her own boxes. That*, my friend, is giving a bitch much needed respect. *Hey, bitch, get away from my bike*. That, my friend, is calling a bitch a bitch."

Smokey narrowed his eyes and stared back at him. "I don't see the difference."

Eddie glanced at me, grinned, and rolled her eyes.

I smiled back at her, then flopped down on the loveseat and waited for the conclusion of the argument.

P-Nut shook his head and then turned toward the kitchen. "You're simple-minded, that's why you ain't seein' it, Smoke. The difference is there."

"Where you going?" I asked.

He glanced over his shoulder. "Gettin' a beer."

Smokey cleared his throat. "I'm not done with this."

"Nothing more to talk about," P-Nut said. "No harm no foul."

While P-Nut got a beer from the fridge, Smokey turned toward me. "Do you like being called a bitch?"

I shrugged. "I don't...it...I..." I widened my eyes and grinned falsely. "It's...I'm okay. It wasn't a big deal."

His lips thinned and he glanced down at the floor. After exhaling through his nose, he looked up. "Do. You. Like. Being. Called. A.

Bitch?"

Oh, wow.

I shook my head. "No."

Smokey turned toward the kitchen and tilted his head back. "You offended her, Nut."

"Sorry, Sandy."

"Bullshit," Smokey said. "Come in here and say it. Doesn't count if you're not looking at her. Apology from the kitchen while you're sipping a beer doesn't count."

"Who the fuck makes up these rules?" P-Nut complained.

"No cussing in the house, P-Nut," Eddie hissed.

I felt like I'd joined the circus. As the sound of someone chugging beer came closer and closer, I glanced over my shoulder.

"Didn't mean to offend you," P-Nut said, wiping his mouth with the back of his hand. "But I wasn't calling you a bitch in the *bitch* context, I was calling you a bitch in the *affectionate* context. Like when people say, *that's my bitch.* Or, *you're my bitch.* In the right context, anything can be said."

"That's okay, it makes sense now that you've explained it."

He tilted his bottle of beer toward Smokey. "I knew you'd understand. He's hard-headed, and he gets mad really easy about dumb shi--" He paused and looked at Eddie. "Dumb *stuff.*"

"I'm standing right here, Nut. I can hear you "

"It was all true, Smoke. You're a hot-head. I'd say it to your face. Hell, I just did."

Smokey waved his hand toward P-Nut and then sat down in the chair in the corner of the room. He looked at Eddie.

Dressed in cut-off jean shorts, Chucks, and a burnout tee, she looked adorable.

"When's Dick get here?" Smokey asked.

Eddie glared at him and let out an exhaustive sigh. "Richard."

He kicked his feet onto the ottoman. "When?"

She shoved her hands in the pockets of her shorts. "7:00-ish."

"Tonight's the night?" P-Nut asked.

Smokey nodded. "First potential date."

"Oh, wow." I looked at Eddie. "Tonight?"

She grinned and nodded. "He's got to come talk to dad first."

"That

"That's exciting," I said.

She wrinkled her nose. "Not really."

"Want some help with your makeup or anything?"

She smiled. "Sure."

"I wouldn't go too far," Smokey said. "They might not be going anywhere."

"Dad!"

"If he's a shit-head, he's not taking you out of this house."

"He's not."

"According to *you*."

"He's on the honor roll."

"Nerds can be shit-heads," Smokey said with a laugh.

"You're impossible," Eddie huffed.

"I'm a realist."

"Can I stay," P-Nut asked. "Just to watch."

"Sure," Smokey said.

"No," Eddie blurted at the same time.

P-Nut shrugged and flopped down on the couch. "Sorry, Ed."

"You guys better be nice to him."

"I'm always nice," P-Nut said. "Your dad's the hot-head."

"Depends on which context you're talking about," Smokey said, his tone thick with sarcasm.

I glanced at the clock.

5:30.

I looked at Eddie and then stood. "Want to start getting ready?"

"What about these boxes?" P-Nut asked jokingly.

I looked at Smokey, winked, and then turned toward P-Nut. "Gotta respect a bitch like me who'll make a prick like you carry her boxes to the bedroom."

He sat up and blinked a few times. "Did you just call me a prick?"

I nodded. "Not a *prick*, prick. But a prick in the not so much a prick sense. I meant prick in an affectionate way. You know, anything can be said if it's done in the right context."

"One point for Sandy, zero for the Nut," Smokey said.

As I walked toward Eddie, she turned toward her room.

"He keeps track of everything," she whispered as I stepped to her side. "And he forgets nothing."

"I'll remember that," I said.

"We're going to have to be conservative on the makeup," she said as we walked into her bedroom. "Or dad will flip out."

"I know a few tricks."

"I wish I knew a trick to make him let me go out with Richard. I'm afraid he's going to be a jerk."

"Maybe he'll surprise you."

"I doubt it," she said.

I on the other hand, reserved hope.

RIGID

Because so far, Smokey had surprised the shit out of me.

TWENTY FOUR

Smokey

When the doorbell rang, I felt sick. It wasn't the kind of sick that a pill or medicine could fix, either. It was fear of the inevitable. Probably the same feeling those sentenced to hang got as they were led to the gallows.

"You want me to get that?"

I swallowed heavily and nodded.

P-Nut pulled the door open.

"Mr. Wallace?"

"Nope. Not Mr. anything." P-Nut stepped to the side. "Get your ass in here and have a seat, son."

Sandy was sitting on the loveseat reading a book, and Eddie was cowering in her bedroom, ashamed of what might happen.

Richard walked in, paused at the edge of the loveseat, and nodded slightly. "Mr. Wallace?"

By my guess, he was six foot tall. His slight build made him seem taller, but when standing beside P-Nut, their height wasn't measurably different. His hair was dark, and kind of all over the place, but a neat mess.

Dressed in khakis, loafers, and a plaid button-down short-sleeved shirt, he looked like a dork.

I stood and extended my hand. "Nice to meet you, Richard. Have a seat."

He sat at the end of the loveseat, turned toward me, and smiled. "I'd like to ask your permission, Sir. I'd like to take your daughter on a date."

P-Nut posted himself up behind the loveseat with his arms crossed, and his eyes fixed on the back of Richard's head.

"How long have you been driving, Richard?" I asked.

He crossed his legs. "Almost two years."

"How long, *legally*? By yourself?"

His shoulders slumped slightly. "Two months."

"You're barely eighteen years old?"

"I turned eighteen two months ago. Yes, Sir."

"Do you live with your parents?"

"Yes, Sir. I sure do."

"Both of them?"

He grinned and nodded. "Yes, Sir."

"What does your mother do for a living?"

"She doesn't work. She looks after my youngest brother, mostly. He's four."

"And, your father?"

He looked embarrassed. "He's the finance manager for BMW in La Jolla."

"Do you drive a BMW?"

His eyes fell to the floor. "No, it's a Mini Cooper."

"Made by BMW, aren't they?"

He shrugged. "I'm not sure."

"If I let you take her on a date, what are your plans?"

"Short term?"

"For the night, Richard." I said, my tone a little harsher than I wanted it to be. "What will you do from the time you leave here, until the time you return?"

"We were going to try and see a movie, if possible."

"That's a bad idea, Richard."

Sandy, who had spent the entire time listening, but acting like she wasn't, lowered her book and began to outwardly pay attention.

Richard did little to hide his disappointment. "Why uhhm. Why is it a bad idea?"

"The movie isn't a good place to get to know someone. Might be good for a third date, but not the first. Hell, you sit for two hours and stare at the screen, and then when it's over, you don't know one single thing about what she likes, doesn't like, or what her taste in music is. If it were me, I'd take her for a cup of coffee, get to know her, and then take her out to the pier to watch the sunset."

He nodded. "Sounds like fun."

Sandy grinned, tilted her book toward her face, and appeared to begin reading again.

I locked eyes with my daughter's potential date. "Let me explain something to you, Richard."

He sat up straight and held my gaze. "Yes, Sir?"

"I've raised that girl since the day she was born. She's a good girl, and by the grace of God, she's never been hurt. No broken limbs, no fractures, no operations, nothing. She's never been hurt by a boy for that matter, either. Until now, her only concern has been her schoolwork. I'm protective of her, Richard."

I leaned forward and rested my forearms on my thighs. "*Very* protective. If I let you take her out, you and I must reach an agreement first."

RIGID

He swallowed hard. "Okay."

"Whatever you do *to* her, *with* her, or *for* her, I want you to stop and think about it before you do it. Ask yourself this: If Mr. Wallace found out *exactly* what I did, would he be a happy man, or would he be an angry man. If the answer is angry, I want you to reconsider doing it. If the answer is happy, proceed, but with caution. Is that understood?"

He sighed. "Yes, Sir."

"Don't make me angry, Richard. No one here wants that, especially you."

"I won't, Sir."

"You're aware she's taken 12 years of Taekwondo, aren't you?"

"I'm aware. Yes, Sir."

"You don't want to make her mad either," I said.

"I won't disappoint either of you."

I stood and extended my hand.

He stood, grinned, and shook my hand. "Thank you, Sir."

"That's it?" P-Nut asked.

I turned up my palms. "That's it."

"Bullshit," P-Nut said.

Before I could object, he came around the corner of the loveseat and shot Richard a laser sharp glare. "Sit down!"

Richard fell into the seat as if he'd been shot.

P-Nut folded his arms across his chest, lowered his chin, and looked down his nose at the kid. "I'm her fucking uncle," he said through his teeth. "Wanna guess what they call me?"

Richard's Adam's apple rose, and then fell. An inaudible *what* puffed from his lips.

"P-Nut. The 'P' is for Percy, and the 'Nut' is because I'm fucking

192

nuts. You so much as touch that girl inappropriately, and *I* hear about it? If you even kiss her on the porch, you're fucked, son. You don't want to piss me off, cause if you do…" He tilted his head toward me. "He'll be the least of your worries. Catch my drift?"

Richard nodded. "Yes, Sir."

"Sir? Did I say my name was 'Sir'?"

"No, P-Nut."

"One kiss on the porch, or if one fucking hair on her head is out of place--"

Eddie's bedroom door opened.

"P-Nut!" she shouted.

P-Nut spun around. An oh *shit look* covered his face.

"Stop it," she barked.

P-Nut looked at her, and then shot Richard a glare. "I meant what I said," he whispered.

Eddie looked at P-Nut and then at me. "What are you two doing? I could hear the cussing in my room."

I shrugged. "I asked him a few questions. P-Nut wanted to say something before you guys left, and things got a little out of hand."

Her eyes went wide. "We get to go? Tonight?"

"Do you have any questions for him, Sandy?"

She tilted her head to the side. "Have fun."

"But not too much," P-Nut said.

"Hold up. Before you go…" I reached for my wallet, opened it, and pulled out a $100 bill. "This one's on me."

He shook his head. "Mr. Wallace, I can't--"

"You can. Just this once."

"Thank you, but I can't. I wouldn't be much of a man if I did."

"Just take it."

"No, Sir. I will not. I'm sorry if you find it offensive, but I find it equally offensive to take it."

Impressive.

"What time will you have her home?"

"Midnight?" he squeaked.

Eddie looked at me with hopeful eyes.

"12:30, and if it's a minute later, you'll not take her out again until she's 18."

"Thank you, Sir."

Sandy grinned.

P-Nut glared.

I let out a sigh. "Have a good time."

On her way to the door, Eddie glanced over her shoulder and mouthed the words *thank you.*

I waved and tried to hide my fear with a smile, but doubted I was a complete success. When the door closed behind them, I walked to where Sandy was sitting and collapsed onto the loveseat beside her.

She set her book to the side, rested her head on my shoulder, and forced her hand between my legs.

With my thigh cupped gently in her hand, she snuggled up against me. "She'll be just fine."

"I sure hope so."

"She will," she said.

"I hope you're right."

"We talked for an hour when I helped her with her makeup."

I sat up and looked at her. "About what?"

She snuggled against me again. "Girl stuff. She'll be fine."

I closed my eyes and allowed Sandy to melt into me while Patrick Sweany's *Your Man* played.

After a few songs, Sandy's weight became heavy. Then, her breathing became soft and predictable. I opened my eyes, glanced at her, and smiled. Across the room, on the edge of the couch, P-Nut sat, snoring like a broken buzz saw.

We were all exhausted from the move, Sandy more so than anyone, and rightfully so.

Filled with concern, I allowed the music to fill me. Oddly, my worries weren't limited to Eddie being on her first date.

I was equally worried about the development of my relationship with Sandy, and of our new baby's health.

Only time would tell if my concerns were without merit, and the one of the best ways I knew to pass time was to sleep.

So, with Sandy and one of my babies in my arms, I closed my eyes and fell asleep.

TWENTY FIVE

Sandy

The first date was *the most amazing day in my life*, according to Eddie. Richard brought her home at 11:45, and when she got there, she stayed up until 1:00 telling Smokey and me about what a great time she had. Richard sounded like a very well-mannered young man, and hearing firsthand how polite and courteous he was did nothing but give peace of mind to both of us.

She was now on date number two with him, and P-Nut sat this one out, which left Smokey and me at home alone. It was our first unaccompanied night together since I moved in, and I was slightly anxious about how it might go.

He sat in his chair, and I sat on the spot I'd claimed on the loveseat, and we were trying to decide what to do with our idle time.

"Pee Bee and Tegan play Scrabble all the time," he said.

"Scrabble?"

"They say it's relaxing, and it sounds like it's pretty funny sometimes

"I'd play Scrabble."

"I don't have it. I'll add it to the grocery list."

It was odd having Smokey do the grocery shopping, but it was something he did, and seemed to enjoy. I hoped, in time, that we could go together.

RIGID

A song I didn't recognize was playing softly in the background. After trying for a moment to listen to the lyrics, I looked at him and grinned a slight smile. "I like listening to the music."

"Can't live without it."

"Why is that?"

"It's relaxing. Music is like soap and water for the soul. I get home from a long day of riding, and I take a shower. If my hands get dirty out in the yard, I wash 'em. What do we do to clean our *insides*, though? Nothing. I listen to music. Every song takes me somewhere different." He glanced around the living room and nodded. "I like it."

"I like it, too. What song is this?"

"It's The Record Company. The song is *On the Move*."

It was a bluesy song with a good beat and a cool harmonica solo. I imagined him fucking me while it played in the background, and got uncomfortably horny at the thought.

"Do you know the names of them all?"

"Most of them."

Since I got pregnant, we hadn't had sex. Being near Smokey for any length of time and *not* wanting to fuck him was impossible. Considering how caring he'd been, and how many times he'd snuck in an unsuspecting kiss, I couldn't help but wonder why we hadn't fucked since trying to make things work out.

I set my book on the coffee table. "I need to go to the bathroom. I'll be right back."

Immersed in the music, he sat in his chair in a trance-like state and nodded lightly.

I went to the bedroom and got undressed. I chose a plaid skirt, knee-high socks, my Chucks, and a white button down shirt, then got dressed.

Feeling good about my decision, I dug through my dresser drawer, found my black horn-rimmed glasses, and put them on.

I got to the door, peered into the living room, and noticed Smokey had gone into the kitchen. After a quick reconsideration, I changed my plans, ditched my panties, and tiptoed into the living room.

"Need anything while I'm in here?" he shouted.

"No, thank you."

His focus was on the small can of almonds he was carrying, and he didn't even notice me. He sat in his chair, poured a few almonds into his palm, and set the can aside.

"You know, these little fuckers are really good for you. They've got…" He looked up. "Jesus."

"What?"

He swallowed heavily. "Goin' somewhere?"

"Nope."

"Oh." He tossed a few of the almonds into his mouth. "What uhhm. Why'd you change?"

I shrugged. "I got tired of the sweats and tee shirt."

He swallowed again.

I turned toward him and wagged my knees back and forth, slowly.

"I didn't realize you wore glasses."

"I don't."

He set the remaining almonds beside the tin and wiped his hand on the thigh of his jeans. "You are."

Using the tip of my index finger, I pushed them up the bridge of my nose. "I just put 'em on when I want to get noticed."

His eyes fell to my feet, then slowly took in every inch of my outfit. He crossed his legs. "What. What about the uhhm." He motioned toward the floor. "What about the socks?"

"They keep my legs warm."

"Are you cold?"

I wagged my knees again, once. "No but I will be."

He fixed his gaze on my nether region, uncrossed his legs and then crossed them again. "Why?"

"When I take off the skirt. My little butt might get cold. The socks will keep my legs warm."

"You uhhm. You plannin' on taking it off, are you?"

I slid the glasses down to the tip of my nose, and peered at him over the top of the frames. "I think I might. There's one good thing about taking it off, though."

He let out an audible breath, then swallowed again. "What's that?"

"I won't have to take off my panties."

He nodded, but it seemed unintentional. Seeing him dressed in his jeans and a wife beater, yet acting so uncomfortable, was rewarding.

And torturous.

"You gonna. You uhhm. You plannin' on leaving them on?" he stammered. "The uhh. The panties?"

Feigning innocence, I pointed toward the bedroom door and wiggled my index finger. "On my way out here. I dropped them on accident. They're on the floor over there."

I crossed my legs, and then uncrossed them, lifting my left leg high enough that he should have been able to see my pussy when I did it.

I was soaked, and wondered if he was as excited as I was. If nothing else, he was terribly uncomfortable, and I was enjoying it.

"The shoes are uhhm. They're cute."

I extended my left leg straight, spread my legs wide, and pointed my foot toward him. "I can get good traction with them."

"Traction?"

I stood, turned toward the loveseat, and bent over.

A heavy sigh shot from his lungs.

I tilted my head to the side, looked at him, and spread my feet wide, stomping them in place onto the hardwood floor. "When I'm getting fucked from behind. They let me stay in one place, and not slide around."

"Jesus."

"What?"

He uncrossed his legs and stood.

Every inch of the outline of his cock was visible through his faded jeans, and it was as hard as a rock.

I stood, turned toward him, and swallowed heavily.

I covered my mouth with my fingertips and twisted my hips back and forth. "Oh. I'm so sorry. I didn't mean to make you uncomfortable."

I lowered myself to my knees, pushed my glasses up my nose, and held out my hands. "Let me see if I can fix that for you. I know a trick."

He took a few steps toward me. "A trick."

I nodded. "Uh huh. Get it out, and I'll show you."

I was surprised there wasn't a puddle on the floor beneath me. I was soaking wet, and felt like I was going to burst into flames. Inches from my grasp, the sexiest man on earth was walking in my direction, and he had a raging stiffy so big it was intimidating.

He stepped in front of me, unbuckled his belt, and unzipped his pants.

His cock rose to attention, then twitched.

I put my hand against my cheek, tilted my head to the side, and acted slightly confused. "If I remember right, you're going to need to put it in my mouth and let me suck on it for a while."

I looked up.

His arms were folded in front of his massive chest. He met my gaze. "If you think it'll work."

"It works best if you talk dirty while I'm doing it."

"Does it?"

I nodded. "Filthy."

I loved dirty talk, and although most women would probably disagree with my taste in sexual banter, the nastier it was the more turned on I got. For me, having my man call me a dirty little whore during the throes of passion was a huge turn on.

But, it only worked with the right guy at the right time.

There was no doubt Smokey was the right guy.

And, the juices that were running along my inner thigh were proof enough that it was the right time.

"How filthy?" he asked.

"I just love being talked dirty to." I glanced at his twitching cock, and then met his downward gaze. "The filthier, the better."

He stroked his hand along the thick shaft. "Put my cock in your mouth."

I cocked my head to the side. "That's not even close."

"Suck my cock," he growled.

Obviously, he needed a little encouragement, so I took a chance. A *big* chance. "Make me," I said. "Or you can go sit your pussy ass down on the couch and whack off."

He grabbed my head in his hands, forced his cock into my mouth, and began to fuck my face like he was ridding himself of a lifetime of anger. "Suck that cock, you mouthy little slut."

My eyes fell closed, and I eagerly accepted every inch of him into

SCOTT HILDRETH

my throat. With each thrust of his hips, he barked out another verbal expression of his deepest desires.

Me?

I was in cock heaven.

With the tip of his dick filling my throat and his hips plastered against my face, breathing wasn't easy. I loved every fucking minute of it.

While I struggled to survive on what little oxygen was in my lungs, continuing all the while to be the little whore that I knew he deserved, he fucked my face it was all that mattered to him. I hoped, at least for that moment, that it was *all that mattered to him.*

When I reached a point that I could take it any longer, I pushed against him and turned my head to the side.

I sucked in a quick breath, hoping he wouldn't give me much time to recover.

He sure didn't.

"I said *suck that cock.*" He guided it past my lips, into my mouth, and commenced to pound himself into my willing throat.

For me, sucking a cock was a much-needed prerequisite to sex. I was already soaking wet before we started, but having a cock against my face made me horny down to my core.

Having Smokey's stiff shaft forced into my mouth was doing a wonderful job of prepping me for a full night of crazy sex, and I was loving every thick inch of it.

And we were just getting started.

As his scent filled my nostrils, he thrust his cock in and out of my mouth with long strokes. With each rearward motion of his hips, he was cautious enough not to allow me to gasp another breath before he pushed it deep into my throat again.

Confused, exhausted, and horny as fuck, I allowed it to continue for as long as I could.

"Gag on that big dick," he growled. "And get those big titties out and squeeze 'em."

As soon as I realized what he'd said, I fumbled to unbutton my top.

"Listen to me, you dirty little slut." His hand gripped my neck. "I told you to squeeze those big titties."

Oh God.

Yes.

With my neck clenched firmly in his hand, he forced his hips against my face, and then ripped my top open. As the buttons scattered across the floor, I yanked my bra down and immediately began fumbling with my hard nipples.

With my head reeling from lack of oxygen, and my pussy on fire, I squeezed my nipples and pulled on my titties.

I was on the verge of a sexual meltdown.

He pulled himself from my mouth.

I gulped a breath, and then another.

I looked up.

He must have seen it in my eyes.

With his eyes locked on mine and the web of his hand beneath my chin, he lifted me to my feet.

My face was sloppy from his assault of my mouth.

He pressed his lips to mine and kissed me savagely.

Oh, God.

Yes.

Yes.

Yes.

His mouth was mashed against mine. Our tongues intertwined.

He pulled away and looked me in the eyes. "Bend over and show me that little pussy."

Telling his blue eyes *no* would have been impossible. When it came to Smokey, however, I was afraid the word *no* would never pass my lips.

My head was spinning. I stumbled to the edge of the couch, hiked my skirt over my hips and spread my feet wide.

"Take it," I breathed. "It's yours."

The pressure of his fingers being shoved inside me caused me to gulp a breath.

"God damned right it is," he said. "*My* pussy."

My eyes fell closed at the thought of him taking possession of me. "Yours."

He worked his fingers in and out of my wetness, the palm of his hand tapping my swollen nub with each stroke.

"Mine," he growled.

Hearing him claim me as his caused me to melt. In response, my clit tingled.

Then, my pussy contracted.

His fingers continued their magic. "Mine," he said. "My fucking pussy."

I bit into my lips and snuck in an orgasm. And then, another.

He leaned over me. With his muscular chest against my back, he pressed his mouth to my ear. "Did you come?"

"I...uhhm...uh huh."

"Don't do it again without permission," he commanded.

His warm breath caused goosebumps to rise along my arms. Then, my legs buckled. I inhaled a choppy breath and offered my apology.

RIGID

"I'm sorry. It won't happen again."

His fingers slipped from inside of me, and although I still felt the tingle from his touch, I yearned for more.

I lifted my head, and glanced over my shoulder.

His fingers twisted into my curly locks, and with my hair gripped tight in his hand, he forced my face against the couch cushion.

I gasped as I felt the pressure of him penetrating me.

My head was spinning. His thick cock seemed to take me places I had never been to, and being there confused me greatly. I focused on the feeling of having him inside of me and tried to escape to a place that allowed me to relish in it.

"Do you like that thick cock?"

The sound of his voice was distant and dull.

I blinked, and prepared to respond.

Whack!

A sharp sting on my right ass cheek caused me to suck in an unexpected breath.

"I asked you a question."

"I love..." I drew another breath. "I love it."

He pushed himself in so deep he bottomed out. "Your tight little pussy feels good."

I clenched my eyes closed. "I love your cock."

"Louder," he said. "Scream it."

"I love your cock!"

It felt good to say it. It felt better to scream it.

His intensity increased. The sound of skin-on-skin drowned out the sound of the music.

"Again," he shouted. "Say it over and over. Who's cock do you love?"

With each stroke, I shouted.

"I love your cock!"

"I love your cock!"

"I love your cock!"

I felt him swell.

Oh, God. Please.

My inner walls clenched him tight.

"I love your cock!" I bellowed. "I love your cock!"

"I love your cock!"

His hips swung back and forth wildly, filling me completely with his thickness.

"I love your cock!"

He pressed himself deep inside and held his hips against my ass.

"I love your cock!"

Oh God.

My pussy contracted, sending a wave of emotion through me. Slowly, he pulled himself from me.

The thought of my impending orgasm escaped me.

I felt the tip of his cock against my wet lips. As he pushed himself back in deep, I recalled the need to ask permission.

"Can I come?"

"You may."

My body shuddered

Every inch of me began to tingle.

Two quick strokes later, and he swelled and became stiff as a stone.

I felt him explode inside of me.

The feeling of his release caused me to do the same.

Together, we reached a climax like no other I'd ever experienced.

"Fuuuuck yesss," he howled.

My legs quivered. With my face buried in the couch cushion, I heaved for each breath. Eventually, I lifted my head and turned to face him.

"You're amazing," I whispered.

"You're mine," he said. "Don't you ever forget that, Sandy."

"Yours." Saying it felt right, so I said it again. "Yours."

"I mean it," he said.

I grinned. "I do, too."

We showered together, and he took special care of me, holding me, kissing me, and insisting that he wash my entire body.

With my back to the shower head, I let the warm water sooth my tired muscles. I closed my eyes as he dabbed me with the soapy loofa.

He snuck an unexpected kiss, and the surprise caused my heart to flutter.

It dawned on me as the water cascaded down upon us that he wasn't the man I thought he was when we met. He was simply protecting what was important to him, and sacrificing who he was to do so.

Now that we were *together*, his true self was shining through.

Attaching myself to Smokey was difficult. Doing so with Grayson Edward Wallace was easy.

All I had to do was open my eyes.

I opened my eyes. "I like you."

He dragged his hands across his hair, turned off the water, and chuckled. "I like you, too."

We got out, dried off, and I got dressed. After fumbling in the closet for a moment, he slipped on a pair of sweats and an old tee shirt.

"You look cute."

"Cute?" He coughed out a laugh. "Thanks."

When we walked into the living room, another blues tune was playing. Once again, I imagined him fucking me to it sometime in the near future.

I paused and cocked my head to the side. "Who is this?"

"The Heavy, *Short Change Hero*," he said.

"How do you remember everything?"

He shrugged. "Mind like a vault."

We each got a bottle of water and he kissed me on the way out of the kitchen. It wasn't aggressive, or extremely passionate, but it was meaningful, and I'd eagerly take as many of them as he wanted to give me.

"7Horse *Meth Lab Zoso Sticker*," he said as we walked into the living room.

Before we got to the couch, the front door opened.

Eddie stepped through the door, walked to the loveseat, and sat down. "Hi."

Smokey turned to face her. "How'd it go?"

She grinned. "Perfect."

"What did you do?"

"Let's see. Pizza, then coffee. Sunset from the pier, then ice cream, and another coffee. Went back to the beach, walked around barefoot, and then here."

"Glad you had fun."

She looked at each of us. "What about you guys?"

He shrugged. "Just listened to music."

She cocked her head to the side. "7Horse." She nodded. "Love this song."

"What is it with you two?" I asked.

"What?" Eddie asked.

"The music. How do you remember all the songs?"

"Seventeen years from now," she said. "And you'll know all of them, too."

I hoped she was right.

And, I was eager to spend the next seventeen years finding out.

TWENTY SIX

Smokey

"I ain't riding with the cocksucker," P-Nut said. "I don't give a fuck."

"He's a good kid." I wiped a few water droplets off the rear fender. "Give him a chance."

He shot me a look. "He ain't got a neck."

I looked the bike over, and then met his gaze. "What does that have to do with anything?"

"I don't trust neckless fuckers."

"You don't trust anyone."

He shrugged. "Trust you."

"Anyone besides me?"

He lit a cigarette, took a drag, and exhaled the smoke through his nose. "I'm thinking not. Other'n Eddie."

"No shit," I said.

I wiped down the gas tank, and took a step back. "Spotless. Once a year, whether it needs it or not."

He took another drag off his cigarette. "Would you let him ride your bike?"

A true biker never let anyone ride his bike that he didn't trust 100%, and I trusted no one 100%, except for P-Nut.

"Fuck no," I responded.

He blew the smoke to the side. "Why not?"

"Don't trust--" I paused, realizing what I was about to say. "That's different."

He shook his head. "Sure as fuck isn't."

"Is too."

"Is not."

"I'd let you ride it," I said.

He clenched the cigarette in his teeth and shrugged. "You *trust* me. That, motherfucker, is my point. You want to tell yourself you trust him, but you don't."

"I just want him to get to know some of the fellas. He's been asking."

"If he's askin' questions, he's probably a cop."

"You think everyone's a cop."

He took a long drag, blew a few smoke rings, and then met my gaze. "Don't think you're a cop."

"He's a Marine. Or, he was. He fought for this country. For our freedom."

He shook his head. "Fuck that. He didn't fight for *me*." He stood up. "Cocksucker didn't fight for me. That fucker don't *know* me. I fight my own fights. Fuck that dude."

I let out a sigh.

He crossed his arms over his chest. "There's lots of cops that are former soldiers and shit. Tell that kid to kick rocks. Question askin' prick."

"All he asked was to meet some of the fellas."

"That's one question too many. Remind him he's a fucking prospect. Or, hell, take him to that Mexican's house. Cholo. Yeah, introduce him to Cholo."

"Cholo's a good motherfucker. Don't talk shit on him."

"Who was talking shit?"

"You called him a Mexican."

He scrunched his nose and stared. "He *is* a Mexican."

"He's Hispanic."

"He's a Mexican."

"Hispanic."

He tossed his cigarette on the floor and pressed the toe of his boot against it. "If you're *Hispanic,* what's your native language?"

I shrugged. "Spanish."

He nodded. "Let's assume a guy down in Tijuana swam over the river, walked to San Diego, and got him a fake Social Security card. Then, let's say he got a job here in Oceanside at the carwash. Then, after working there for a couple of years, he bought it." He spread his arms wide and gazed up at the ceiling as if looking up at a marquee. "Called it Pepe's Car wash."

I narrowed my eyes and shook my head. "You gonna make a point?"

"I was tryin'," he said. "Lemme finish."

"Finish."

"Would Pepe be white?"

"No."

"What would he be?'

"Hispanic."

He nodded. "Hispanic?"

"Yep."

"Where did he come from?"

"Tijuana, according to you."

"What country is Tijuana in?"

"Mexico."

"Who lives in Mexico?"

"Mexicans."

"Pepe's a Mexican, then."

"Once he crosses the border, he's Hispanic."

"Whatever," he said. "Take that question askin' prospect over to your Hispanic buddy's house. They can eat tamales together."

"Stop being a prick."

"Oh, now you gonna tell me that Cholo don't eat tamales? Hell, *I* eat tamales, so I know he eats em. They're good as fuck."

"Just forget it."

"Forgotten."

I tossed my rag on the toolbox. "You ready?"

He looked up. "Ready to what?"

"Ride?"

"Just you and me?"

I nodded. "Yep."

He picked up his cigarette but, twisted it between his fingers, and sprinkled loose tobacco all over my spotless bike. "Sure," he said. "Let's roll. Where we headed?"

"What the fuck are you doing?" I snarled.

"Looks funny bein' all clean. I was just doin' you a solid," he said.

I shook my head. "Figured we'd eat lunch. I was thinking Mexican food."

"Where we going?" he asked with a laugh. "Hispanico?"

TWENTY SEVEN

Sandy

I was comfortable in my new home when Smokey was present, but when he was gone, I felt out of place. As if I was invading space that I didn't have the right to, I reluctantly opened each of the drawers, looking for the silverware while Eddie took a shower.

I realized as I pulled open drawer after drawer, that although I'd been in the house for two weeks, I didn't know where the silverware was.

On the next to the last drawer, I hit the jackpot.

Thank God.

I grabbed a butter knife, and closed the drawer.

Did I just see what I thought I saw?

I opened it again.

I gazed at the silverware, which was situated in a wooden cutlery organizer. Beside the organizer were three pairs of chopsticks. I smiled and shut the drawer.

I got the bread from the pantry, some ham, the cheese, and then looked for the mayonnaise. While scanning the compartments on the refrigerator doors, I saw another surprise.

I picked up the bottle.

Sandwich Pal Horseradish Sauce.

I grinned and closed the drawer.

RIGID

I made my sandwich, and spread a thick layer of horseradish sauce on the bread. As I ate, I decided to make a mental list of all the things about Smokey that I didn't like. By the time I was finished eating, I hadn't come up with one single thing. On my way to the sink, I came up with no less than six things about him that I did like.

Convinced that I could fall in love with him if he could fall in love with me, I washed my hands and walked into the living room.

Eddie was relaxing on the couch with her Kindle.

"Oh," I said. "I thought you were in the shower."

"I was," she said. "Not anymore, though."

"When does your dad get home most of the time?"

"On Saturday?" She shrugged. "Before dinner."

"I didn't have to work, so I'm just kicking it."

She looked up. "We can kick it together. If you want."

I sat down. "Okay."

She tossed the tablet to her side and sighed. "I've got a lot left to read."

"What are you reading?"

"I like NA stuff."

"NA?"

"New Adult."

"What's that?"

"It's a genre about kids my age. Leaving home. Relationships. Finding a job. College. Just stuff like that, but it always includes falling in love."

"Sounds fun."

"NA, or falling in love?"

I shrugged one shoulder. "Both."

"It's fun to think about."

"Falling in love?" I asked.

She nodded. "Yeah."

"Is Richard the one?"

"I don't know. He's cool, and we have fun together, but who knows."

I wondered if she was being totally truthful with me and quickly decided she probably wasn't. I doubted she trusted me, for one, and secondly, I suspected she thought I'd tell her father anything she told me.

I wondered about developing a friendship with her, and wondered if I could so and maintain some level of separation as a parent.

"Are uhhm. Are you and your dad friends?"

She looked at me like my head was on fire, and then laughed. "Yeah. Like, *best friends*."

"That's cool," I said.

"What about your dad and you?" she asked.

"He left when I was little."

Her nose wrinkled. "That sucks. What about your mom?"

"She uhhm. She was…she *is* a drug addict. I left home when I was thirteen and moved in with my aunt and uncle. So, I really didn't spend a lot of time around her."

Her eyes dropped to the floor. "My mom was, too. She died."

"I'm so sorry."

She shrugged. "That's what happens. I mean, it sucks, but it happens. Drugs are stupid. I'm glad her and my dad got together, even if it was just for a little while. I mean, if they didn't, I wouldn't be here, you know. So, *that's* cool. But yeah. Drugs are stupid."

"They sure are."

RIGID

She scooched toward the arm of the couch and then turned to face me. "Are you excited about the baby?"

Her eyes made her level of excitement clear, which shocked me. I smiled. "I am. More every day."

She rubbed her hands together. "What do you want?"

"Oh. I don't know. I just want a healthy baby."

"Everybody says that." She chuckled. "You have to want one or the other a little more. Which one? I want a baby sister."

Hearing her say *sister* made me feel like she'd truly accepted the situation wholeheartedly. "Are you excited about being a sister?"

"Oh, man. Am I? Yeah, I've always wanted to have brothers and sisters, but not so much brothers. Unless I already have a sister, that is. Either would be cool, though."

"I think I'd like a daughter," I whispered. "But don't tell your dad."

"I think he wants a boy." She pressed her index finger against her lips. "I'm not saying a word."

I widened my eyes and shook my head. "I don't want to make him mad."

"Girl power." She raised her hand and turned her palm to face me.

I slapped my hand against hers. "Girl power."

"This is going to be so cool," she said. "When can we find out what the sex is?"

"Like three months or so."

"I can't wait."

I was excited too, but the longer we talked the more excited I became. After half an hour of talking about babies, we were in the kitchen making milkshakes and discussing the fallacy of love.

Eddie took a slurp of her milkshake, and then wiped the corners of her mouth with the tip of her finger. "Love? I think initially that it's a conscious acceptance of a person being satisfactory. You know, as far as *attraction* goes. *Yeah, this guy's hot*, or whatever. So, the girl decides she's attracted to said person, and she gives him a chance." She shrugged. "Then, they hang out. He thinks she's cool, she thinks he's cool, and they bone or whatever. He decides he likes boning her, she knows she likes boning him, and one day he pulls a douche move, and they break up."

She gulped another drink of her milkshake. "Happens all the time. Anyway. Then, she thinks about being with him, and how cool it was to lay around and watch Netflix on the couch. And she tries to forget about him, all she can remember is what it was like when they boned. So, she sends him a text and says, *what's up?* He's watching football with his brahs, and he sees the text and says, check this out. Talia sent me a text. His buddies say, brah, you should so go bone her. When the football game is in the fourth quarter, dude sends her a text and says, not much, wanna hang out? And she gets all excited, and they hang out and bone again. The next day, they declare they're in love."

I chuckled. "Just like that?"

"Mmhhmm." She twirled the spoon around in her cup, decided it was empty, and pushed it to the side. "Just like that."

"You don't think people see each other and just *know*?" I asked.

She dropped her spoon in the sink. After tipping the cup upside down and tapping her hand against the bottom a few times, she scrunched her nose and tossed the cup in the sink, too. She looked up. "Like insta-love?"

"Yeah, basically."

"Nope." She shook her head slowly. "It's written in books, but it's crap. Basically, the same as a unicorn or a vampire. If I read a book, and it's insta-love? I return it and read something else. If I wanted to read a fairy tale, I would."

"People don't just *fall in love*?"

"No. It happens like I said a minute ago."

"Every time?"

"Yeah, pretty much," she said. "Why, how do you think it works?"

I shrugged. I believed in fairy tales. Or, at least I had in the past. "I'm not sure. I think people are attracted to each other, and then they spend time together. They either fall in love, or they don't. If they do, I think it grows over time. If they don't, they move on and try it with someone else."

"Basically, that's what I said. Mine's more realistic, though."

Taking advice on life from Eddie seemed odd, but I liked her concept. "How are you so smart for a seventeen-year-old?"

"I read a lot," she said. "And, I've got a cool dad."

"Yeah. He's pretty cool."

"So are you," she said. "I gotta go poop."

I chuckled as she walked away.

As she took care of her business, I had to wipe away a tear. I told myself it was an estrogen overload.

But, it may have been that I was falling in love a little bit with Eddie, too.

TWENTY EIGHT

Smokey

"I'm not afraid to leave, I've done it plenty of times, but I don't like the thought of leaving on a Saturday night. Especially when she's going out with Richard."

Sandy shook her head adamantly. "Don't worry. I mean it, I'll wait up, just like we do when you are home. And, I'll set the alarm, just like you do. She'll be fine. We'll be fine."

I didn't like leaving Eddie, nor did I like leaving Sandy.

"I don't have to like it," I said. "And, to be straight with you, I don't like leaving you, either."

Her face went flush. "That was sweet."

"Wasn't meant to be sweet," I said. "I'm just telling you how I feel."

She glared playfully. "Well, it was sweet."

I wagged my eyebrows.

"Do you have a say?" she asked. "Can you stay home?"

I shook my head. "It's mandatory. I have no choice."

"Then go, and have fun. Eddie and I will both be fine."

I leaned over the edge of the table. "Come here."

She did the same, and met me in the center of the table.

I kissed her. It seemed to happen a lot more lately, and I was growing to like it much more than I ever would have guessed. Kissing was something that had been missing from my life, and experiencing it was something that seemed to draw me closer to Sandy each day.

So, I decided to kiss her as much as possible.

"I like it when you kiss me," she said.

"Makes two of us. I like kissing you."

She wiped her mouth with her fingertips. "Don't worry about anything. I'll text you every few hours if you want."

"How about every hour, on the hour?"

"Okay."

"I've got a few rules that need to be followed," I said. "I meant to go over them with you before now, but I guess I forgot."

"What are they?"

"Cops show up for *any* reason, no matter what they say, don't let them in the house unless they have a search warrant."

"How do I know if they have one?"

"You ask to see it."

"And, if they don't have one?"

"You tell them to leave."

"Is there. I mean, is there stuff in here that--"

"It's the principle. No, there's nothing illegal in this home. And, I have nothing to hide. But. I'm not letting some shit hat cop come in here and plant any evidence. That's the last thing I need, is to be doing a dime for something I didn't do."

"What's *a dime*?"

"Ten year bit."

"Oh my God," she gasped. "They'd do that?"

"They do it all the time."

"Okay, no coming inside without a search warrant. What else?"

I reached in my pocket, pulled out my pistol, and set it on the table. After opening the cylinder, I unloaded it, and showed her that all five shells were on the table.

"Empty. You see where they go?"

She nodded. "Uh huh."

I handed it to her. "Here."

"Oh wow," she said. "It's heavy."

"Has to be. It's a .357 magnum. If it wasn't, it'd kick so hard it'd break your wrist."

"What's a .357 magnum?"

"It's the shell size. Like a .38 special, only longer."

"Oh."

"It's what they call a double action," I explained. "All you do is point it, and pull the trigger. There's no safety, no switches, no nothing. Just point, and pull the trigger."

"Okay."

I pointed to the left side of the pistol. "Push the lever on the side there, by your thumb, and tilt the pistol to the left."

She did as I asked, and the cylinder fell open.

"See that all five holes are empty?"

She looked at the cylinder. "Uh huh."

"It holds five bullets, that's all. With all five holes open, it can't do anything, okay?"

"Okay."

"Push the cylinder closed."

She closed the cylinder and looked at me.

"Point it at the refrigerator and pull the trigger."

"Are you sure?" she asked.

I nodded. "It's unloaded."

She squinted, and slowly squeezed the trigger. When the pistol dry fired, she jumped.

"It's that simple," I said. "Now, it's got a 2" barrel. You can't really *aim* it, so I'm not going to explain all of that to you. If you ever have to use it, you hold it in your hand just like you are, and you point it, just like your pointing your finger. If you can point your finger at something, you can point the gun at something. Make sense?"

"Uh huh."

"Point it at the sink."

She pointed it at the sink.

"Point it at the trash can."

She did the same.

I turned up my palms. "It's that easy."

"Here are the rules about guns."

She set the gun aside, and looked at me.

"Never, under any circumstances, point a gun, *any* gun, at something you aren't 100% comfortable shooting."

She swallowed heavily, and then nodded. "Okay."

"No matter what."

"Okay."

"Once you've made the decision that you're going to point it at someone, you've got one of two situations. The first is this: you need to shoot, and there's no time for demands. In that case, you do *not* hesitate, you shoot. Hesitation will cost someone's life. Shoot first, make up a story to cover your ass later. The second is this: You want someone to do something. If that's the case, you point the gun, and give your demand. For instance, a man is raping a chick behind a trash dumpster. I'll pull the gun and say, get off of her and get on the ground. If he complies, great. If not, I've got a decision to make. Either way, I'm prepared to shoot, and we know that because why?"

She sat up straight. "Because you pointed it?"

I leaned over and kissed her. "You're a quick learner."

"So, that sums it up. Don't point it unless you are mentally prepared to shoot it, and don't hesitate if there's a life at stake."

"Got it."

"I'm going to load it now. When I leave, it'll be loaded. Leave it that way, and only get it out of the dresser drawer if you have to. It's not an illegal weapon, but it's not registered to me, either. It's just easier that way. If the cops ever do a trace on it, it won't come back to me."

"Okay. What about you? What if--"

I raised my fists. "I've got *these*."

She sighed. "I like your hands. And your little tattoo flowers. Don't hurt them."

"I'll do my best."

"Don't let anything happen to my three babies."

She looked at me and squinted her eyes. "Three?"

I nodded. "You, Eddie, and little man."

She grinned. "I won't."

My gut told me I could trust her.

So, that's what I did

TWENTY NINE

Sandy

Dressed in a pair of boxer shorts I found in the dresser, and one of Smokey's wife beaters, I danced around the house without a bra or panties.

It felt so good to *let go* for once.

I'd loaded the music app on my phone for Smokey's *Sonos* system, and now I could see the names of the songs that played. I wrote down the titles and artists of the ones I liked, and skipped the stupid ones.

After an hour of dancing, I was exhausted.

One chocolate milkshake later, and I was missing Eddie, and even more so, Smokey. Knowing a nap was imminent, I set the alarm for 12:00, and changed clothes into something a little more appropriate, just in case Richard decided to come inside.

After P-Nut's speech, he hadn't so much as walked her to the door. I felt bad for not remembering to say that P-Nut was full of shit, but I figured I could tell him some other time.

I sat on the couch. As Band of Skulls, *Cold Fame* played, I closed my eyes.

I woke up confused.

Still groggy, but fairly certain that I'd heard something, I lifted my head and looked around the house.

RIGID

Nothing.

I couldn't decide if it was a dream. I rubbed my eyes and looked around the room, sure I'd heard someone screaming. I stood up, shook my head, and checked the clock.

11:47.

I heard a dull thud. Then, another. And, another.

I looked for my phone, couldn't find it, and tip-toed toward the Sonos player. After pausing the music, I stood still and listened. My own heartbeat was all I could hear.

Then, the sound of muffled grunts from outside sent chills along my spine.

It sounded like it was right outside the door.

I ran to the bedroom, opened the dresser drawer, got the gun, and rushed to the living room window. After a deep breath, I pulled the blind to the side and peered out into the dark.

I didn't immediately see anything. I scanned the yard from left to right. Then, I saw *everything.*

No.

No.

Oh my fucking God.

No.

I ran to the door, yanked it open, and leaped onto the porch.

What I feared was happening *was* happening.

My stomach heaved. The taste of bile rose in my throat.

I opened my mouth, but no words came. Not so much as a squeak.

Never, under any circumstances, point a gun, any gun, at something you aren't 100% comfortable shooting.

I raised the pistol, and quickly realized they were way too far away.

228

I opened my mouth again.

Nothing.

At the end of the driveway, the devil himself was sitting on top of Eddie. His hands were swinging wildly, and he was beating her like he was trying to kill her. What little noise she had been making only a few seconds prior had ceased.

Panic shot through me, all but crippling me.

His fists crashed down against her face, one after the other. Then he yanked on her hand, lifting her torso from the driveway each time he pulled against it.

Seeing it was killing me inside. I couldn't think, I couldn't speak, and I was shaking like I was naked in Antarctica.

Motherly instinct took over. Without thought or hesitation, I ran off the porch and burst out across the yard in a dead run. Smokey's words ran through my mind.

You want someone to do something. If that's the case, you point the gun, and give your demand.

"Hey motherfucker!" I half screamed, half blubbered. "Get off my daughter!"

He glanced at me, and then yanked against her hand again.

When I reached them I could clearly see that Eddie was *not* okay. On her back, and either unconscious or dead, she wasn't moving. The man on top of her seemed to be in another world, and continued pulling against her hand.

Beside her, a cellphone lay on the concrete.

If you can point your finger at something, you can point the gun at something.

I pointed the pistol at his head.

RIGID

He looked right at me.

Hesitation will cost someone's life.

Shoot first, make up a story to cover your ass later.

I looked him in the eyes. All the fear escaped me. I squeezed the trigger.

A blinding flash of light and a horrific boom happened at the same time.

Somehow, I was no longer holding the pistol.

I looked around me and realized I couldn't see very well. The flash had come close to blinding me. Sobbing, I fell to my knees, and crawled toward the outline of the bodies.

My sight slowly returned, and it was clear her attacker was dead. Half of the lower portion of his face was missing.

And, Eddie wasn't moving.

I shoved the dead man off her, leaned down, and wiped her blood-soaked hair away from her face. "Eddie?"

Her eyes were swollen shut, and her face was a battered mess.

A gurgling sound came from deep inside her throat. "My…ring…"

She's alive.

Thank God.

I blindly searched for the phone that was beside her, picked it up, and dialed 911.

I wasn't a doctor, but I knew if an ambulance didn't come quickly, I'd lose her.

"911 please state the nature of your emergency."

There was only one way I knew to get an ambulance, and get it quick. But, it would require me to tell a lie.

And, just this once, it was okay to lie.

I cleared my throat. "Uhhm. A police officer has been shot, and he's wounded. Send an ambulance. He's dying."

"Your location?"

I had no idea what my new address was.

I glanced toward the porch light.

10378.

"10378 La Quinta," I said.

"Ma'am, can you provide a description of the shooter? Is he still on the scene…"

I threw the phone in the driveway, laid down at Eddie's side, and held her in my arms.

"It's okay, baby. Help is on the way."

It had only been a matter of seconds, but I could already hear the approaching sirens.

"Hear that, baby? They're coming to take you to the doctor. After you get cleaned up, we'll have milkshakes."

"My…ring…" she murmured, her voice almost inaudible.

I sat up and then looked at her swollen hand.

The ring was gone.

I stood, looked around, and saw it glistening between me and the dead piece of shit who tried to rob her.

I picked it up, and tried to slip it on her hand, but her fingers were far too swollen.

"I've got it, baby. I've got the ring," I whispered.

The side of my car illuminated from the flashing lights from the approaching police and ambulance.

In an instant, there were police officers everywhere.

There was no way I could let anything happen to her ring. She'd almost lost her life trying to keep it.

I slipped it on my finger, stood, and waved my arms back and forth. "Here! I need you right here!"

Ambulance attendants rushed into the yard at the same time the police officers did.

Everyone was screaming, and asking questions, but no one questioned whether or not Eddie needed help. It was the first thing that happened.

As they loaded her on the stretcher, I leaned over her. "I love you. You'll be just fine, my baby. I promise." I kissed her forehead, pulled away, and then pressed my hand to hers. "Girl Power."

Upon saying those words, tears ran down along each side of my nose.

Then, everything went black.

THIRTY

Smokey

Attending club functions wasn't my bag of tricks, but when the club needed muscle, I was always willing to show up. More accurately, I wasn't willing, I insisted on it. I had yet to miss any event that required a patch to intimidate, beat, or threated the life of anyone who the club decided needed it.

Standing around an old warehouse with 200 of So-Cal's finest 1%ers, I stood amidst the only bunch I cared much for, the Hells Angels.

One of Hells Angels senior members, Bama, and Pee Bee were talking about the day Pee Bee's father had a heart attack. On that day, Bama had gathered all the Angels at the rally, and led the way on a 150-mile trek to the hospital, providing an escort for the entire trip.

Bama stroked his long gray beard. "That family in the fuckin' Chrysler Magnum was what I thought was funny."

"The white one?" Pee Bee asked.

Bama nodded. "When we shot past him, he swerved so hard his tires smoked and his fuckin' eyes were like *this*."

He went wide-eyed and then looked hard to the left.

"That was funny as shit," Pee Bee agreed.

"You alright, Brother?" Bama asked. "You look sick."

I nodded. "I'm good. Just..."

I took a long breath, exhaled, and then met his gaze. "Nothing big. Daughter's on a date, and my Ol' Lady was supposed to call every hour. She hasn't called in three."

He looked at his watch. "It's 2:00 a.m., Brother. Hell, they're sleeping."

I nodded. "She'll wish she'd called when I talk to her next."

He coughed a laugh. "I know that's right. How old's the daughter?"

"Seventeen."

He stroked his beard and then shook his head. "When Harley was that age, it drove me nuts. Tough age for girls."

"Tough age for all of us," I said.

He gave a nod. "Amen to that."

While Crip finished rubbing elbows with the other club's decision makers, we talked about everything under the sun. the conversations had gone from fucking to food, back to fucking, and then landed on street races.

"I need a set of cams," I said. "Bad."

"What's in her now?" Bama asked.

"Andrews A2," I said.

"Shit, that fucker's flat on the top end. You need to go with something that's got a better horsepower reading. The A2's got torque, but that's about it."

"Tell me about it," I said.

My phone buzzed, and I about jumped out of my skin. I held up my index finger. "Here's that call," I said. "Better late than never."

I pulled my phone from my pocket, looked at the screen, and although the number was local, I didn't recognize it.

I swiped my thumb across the screen. "Smokey."

"Grayson Wallace?"

"Who's this?"

"Is this Grayson Wallace?"

"Depends. Who's this?"

"Sir, this is Dr. Levinson at Scripps Mercy Hospital. Can you provide a Social Security number and any identifying scars or birthmarks for Eddie Cassandra Wallace?"

My heart sank, and panic shot up my throat.

I turned away from the men, and began walking away.

I swallowed hard. "Is she…is she okay?"

"Sir, I need to know if you can provide--"

"She has. She's got. No scars. A dime sized birthmark on her left thigh. Social is. It's uhhm. 514-82-3060."

He shuffled some paperwork. *"And, she's your daughter?"*

"Yes, she is. Is she okay?"

"She's going in to surgery prep right now. We'll likely operate within 30 minutes. If everything goes well, we expect her to recover fully. If at all possible, you need to get her as soon as possible. The procedure is rather complicated. Her skull is fractured, and her brain has swollen considerably. We've drilled holes to relieve the pressure, but we're not seeing the results we'd like to."

My hands began to shake uncontrollably. "What…where…where do I come to?"

"Scripps Mercy in San Diego. Ask for the trauma operating room."

"I can call this number if need be?"

"Yes, this will ring the trauma desk."

"What. What happened?"

"She was assaulted and beaten severely. She's got a few broken

fingers, her forearm is fractured, and several lacerations. I'll forewarn
you. You won't recognize her."

My blood was boiling, and I was shaking so bad I could barely hold
my phone.

"What. What about her uhhm. Her mother?"

"Sir, I'm not at liberty to give out…"

"Is she okay?"

"Sir. You'll have to speak to the police to obtain that information."

I swallowed hard. "Do you have a wife?"

"I do."

"I'll ask again. Is her mother okay?"

He sighed. *"She's been taken into custody."*

"What?"

"That's all I'm comfortably saying at this time."

"She wasn't. She wasn't at. It wasn't her fault? Was it?"

"Mr. Wallace, the only reason your daughter is alive and in good
hands is because of your wife. I suggest you hurry, Mr. Wallace."

"Thank you."

I was an emotional wreck. I turned toward Pee bee and Bama, but
couldn't speak. I needed to get to Scripps Mercy ASAP, but my bike was
a turd, and had no top speed to speak of. If I was forced to ride it, I might
not make it in time.

We were fifty miles away, and getting anyone to give up their sled
wasn't going to happen, and I knew it.

"What is it, Brother?" Bama asked.

I swallowed hard, and gathered every ounce of courage I could
muster. "Daughter's been assaulted, and she's knocking on death's door.
They're uhhm. They're going to cut into her brain. And, I don't know

what's going on, but they got my Ol' Lady in custody, but it sounds like she might have saved my daughter's life."

I looked away and shook my head. After regaining my composure, I turned to face him. "I need to get to Scripps Mercy in SD quick."

"Angels!" Bama shouted at the top of his lungs. "Saddle up."

He looked at me. "We've got your back, brother."

"Might have to ride bitch," I said. "My shit's slow as fuck, Brother."

Pee Bee grabbed my shoulder. "Crip's bike is the fastest motherfucker in the club. Hold on."

I nodded, and he took off through the crowd.

Hells Angels came out of every crack and crevice, and then rushed out the building behind Bama.

Prepared to ride on the back of one of HA's bikes, I stood like a complete idiot, feeling helpless and incapable. Worry for Eddie, and for Sandy filled me until I was sure I would burst.

Crip rushed to my side. "Something happen to Eddie?"

I couldn't respond. I struggled to swallow, and then nodded.

He held out his hand. "Take mine. It'll outrun anything here, Brother."

I reached in my pocket, pulled out my keys, and handed them to him.

He patted me on the shoulder. "Love ya, Brother."

I swallowed hard and nodded.

The building began to shake from the rumbling of bikes outside the doors.

"Pee Bee and Cholo's coming with," Crip said. "I'll go, but your sled won't come close to keeping up."

I nodded and somehow managed to speak. "Understood."

"I'll be right behind you," Crip said.

Pee Bee stepped to my side, and Cholo was right behind him.

"Scripps?"

I nodded.

We rushed out of the building.

At the edge of the parking lot was a line of roughly a dozen bikes. Beside the line and in front, Bama sat on his bagger, revving the engine. "Who's leading this parade?" he shouted.

"The Filthy Fucker's will lead the way," Pee Bee said. "We've got the fastest shit."

I hopped on Crips bike, fired it up, and pulled alongside Bama, who was out in front.

"Red and White!" Bama bellowed over the sound of the exhaust. "Keep up if you can. If you can't keep up…"

He paused and leaned to the side. "What's your daughter's name?"

"Eddie," I said. "Eddie Wallace."

"Her name's Eddie Wallace," he yelled.

Engines revved in response.

Cholo and Pee Bee pulled up to either side of me.

Pee Bee looked at me. "Let's do this."

I bit into my lips and nodded.

And we rode out of there like a bat out of hell.

THIRTY ONE

Sandy

A nice-looking man dressed in a suit walked into the room. "Miss West, I'll be your legal counsel. My name is Jay Parsons."

"Okay."

He set his briefcase on the table. "Can I get you anything?"

"I'm okay."

"Miss West, you've been through a horrific event. Are you alright to talk about it for a moment?"

"Uh huh."

He sat down. "Explain what happened. Can you do that?"

"Can I tell you the truth?"

He nodded. "Please do."

"A man was uhhm. He was beating on Eddie. And I uhhm. I shot him."

"Who is Eddie?"

"My uhhm. She's. She's my boyfriend's daughter."

"Live in boyfriend?"

"Yes. And, my baby's father."

Taking notes as we spoke, he looked up. "A different child?"

"The one in my tummy."

"You're pregnant?"

239

"Uh huh."

"By Eddie's father?"

"Uh huh."

"Continue."

"That's it. I shot him. Then, I called the police."

"Where did you get the gun?"

I'd already considered that I would be asked the question, and considering what Smokey said about the gun not being able to be traced to him, I decided to tell another small lie.

"It was beside the man who attacked her. It must have been his."

He nodded. "And you picked it up?"

"I did."

"Did you command that he stop assaulting her?"

I shook my head. "He wasn't assaulting her. He was beating her with his fists. And bashing her head on the concrete."

"The report states that you commanded that he stop. Is that correct?"

"I did."

"And, when he didn't, you feared for your life, your unborn baby's life, and the life of your step-daughter? Correct?"

I liked him already. "Yes, Sir."

He looked at his notes, and then some printed reports. "At what point did he brandish the knife?"

"Knife?"

He nodded and held up a report. "Yes. The knife that was found on his person."

"I'm uhhm. I'm confused."

"I'm sure you are, Miss West. Not to bore you with details, but California Penal Code 198.5, otherwise known as the Castle Doctrine, allows you to defend yourself when you fear that your life is in danger in your home. The home, by definition, extends to include your yard, driveway, etcetera."

"Okay."

"Words like *I feared for my life, he reached for the knife*, or *he reached for his waistband*? They're all phrases that are historically used in support of the aforementioned penal code."

I nodded. "Okay."

"So, where were we? He had a knife and there was a pistil at his side, correct?"

Shoot first, make up a story to cover your ass later.

I took a deep breath and then let it out. "I came outside. He had a knife in his hand. I yelled for him to stop. He didn't. He hit her over and over. I rushed to help, and there was a pistol beside them on the driveway. He raised his hand, and the knife was in it. I thought he'd kill Eddie for sure. So, I picked up the pistol and yelled for him to stop. He looked right at me, then he started to drive his fist downward. I feared for my life, and the life of my children. I closed my eyes, and pulled the trigger. Then, I blacked out until I got to the police station."

He grinned and nodded his head. "Can you recite that exact statement?"

"I think so."

"No matter who asks you, that is *exactly* what happened. You do not recall any more. And, certainly do not exclude any details."

"Okay. Can I talk to Smokey? I need to know if Eddie's okay."

"Who might Smokey be?"

"Eddie's father. My boyfriend."

"Sure. Do you know his telephone number?"

I didn't. Not by memory.

"I guess not."

"Did you have your phone in your possession?"

"No. I don't know where I left it. It's in the house."

He glanced at his notes. "Well, typically at night, and especially on a Saturday, there's no court, and no available judges or prosecutor's. In this particular case, however, I suspect they'll need to make some special arrangements."

"I don't understand."

"Miss West, you've committed no crime. I'm going to leave here for a moment, and I'm going to call Judge Wardmeier at home, and explain the situation. If they do not release you, without charges, I will file suit against the department, the city, the arresting officers, the prosecutor, and the judge."

"What does that mean for me? Can I talk to Smokey soon?"

"Let me make that call, Miss West. I should have you out of here within the hour."

"Do you know what time it is?"

He looked at his watch. "2:05."

I hadn't called Smokey in three hours.

He was going to be worried for sure.

I lowered my head. "Okay."

***

"Miss West, this is detective Watson. He's got a few things to say, and then you're free to go."

"Miss West. I'm sorry for the inconvenience, but we simply needed to question you. There may or may not be questions that need to be answered in the future. If they come up, I'll contact Mr. Parsons, and we'll go from there. Again, sorry for the inconvenience."

I looked at Mr. Parsons.

He grinned.

I couldn't believe it. To describe everything that had happened as surreal wouldn't even come close.

I looked at detective Watson. "Okay."

"No hard feelings?"

I shook my head and forced myself to grin. "No. Can you tell me where Eddie is?"

"Scripps Mercy," he said.

"Thank you."

"You're quite welcome."

He took the handcuffs, and then left the room.

"That was without incident," Mr. Parsons said. "You're free to go."

"Can I get a ride?"

"Absolutely," he said. "Where?"

"Scripps Mercy?"

"Certainly."

***

Traveling well in excess of 100 miles an hour, we sped down highway 5, toward Scripps Mercy in San Diego. Through Mr. Parsons persuasive tactics, I'd learned that Eddie was scheduled to have surgery at 3:00 am.

At 2:45 in the morning, traffic was sparse. On the highway ahead of us, a long line of taillights from two lines of motorcycles stood out against the otherwise dark stretch of road.

Mr. Parsons changed lanes.

As we passed the bikers, I looked at each of them. I had hoped one might be Smokey, but realized it was wishful thinking.

RIGID

I was sure he'd been contacted by the hospital, and was probably there already. Five or so minutes later, we came up behind four more motorcycles. Naturally, I looked out the window as we approached them.

"These guys are *really* moving," Mr. Parsons said. "I'm going 120."

"Holy crap," I said.

Traveling at roughly the same speed, we slowly crept past them. One of the bikers, who was riding an old-school shitty Harley, reminded me of Smokey.

I did a double take.

In the dark, and with him wearing a helmet and glasses, it was hard to tell. But, it could have been his twin. He even had flowery hand tattoos.

As much as I liked to tell myself I was okay, I wasn't. I was still out of it, and in somewhat of a trance-like state.

I'd been through a lot, and suspected it might even take months for me to recover from the trauma.

"Uhhm. Can you slow down? I want to see those bikers again."

"Do you think one of them might be your boyfriend?"

"I don't know."

We were only a few feet ahead of them, and when he slowed down, they promptly caught up with us.

I turned, pressed my hands to the glass, and stared.

Illuminated by what little light came from behind them, I could clearly see the back of their kuttes. One said *Hells Angels*, and the other three said *Filthy Fuckers*.

My heart raced. I unbuckled my seatbelt and slapped my hands against the glass.

Oh my God.

"It's him!"

My heart surged.

I waved my hands frantically. After a moment, the Hells Angel, who was closest to me, looked in my direction.

"Smokey!" I screamed.

I was sure he couldn't hear me. Nonetheless, I yelled again. And then, again.

The Hells Angel decelerated. Beside him, on a shitty motorcycle, was Smokey.

I filled with emotion, and within a few seconds, tears streamed down my face.

The Hells Angel gave a hand signal, and Smokey glanced toward me.

I grinned, pointed at the road ahead, and mouthed the word *hospital*.

He nodded and fixed his eyes on the road.

"I won't need to call Smokey now," I said. "He's beside us. Can we uhhm. Can we just stay right here? Beside them?"

He nodded. "Sure. We'll be there in five minutes."

They were the longest five minutes of my life.

THIRTY TWO

Smokey

The bond between a parent and their child is beyond compare. Flat on her back with her head wrapped tight in bandages, there was no doubt that Eddie was in pain.

She couldn't tell me how much she was hurting.

Therefore, the pain I felt for her was excruciating.

My knee was bouncing up and down at an impossible rate.

Side by side, Sandy and I sat on a small loveseat beside the bed. After a moment, her hand rested against my thigh, and, at least for that instant, the bouncing stopped. I looked at her and did my best to smile. She did the same, but she couldn't hide her fear. Neither of us could.

Eddie's operation was cancelled after a specialist reviewed her condition. All we could do was wait for the swelling to go down. In a drug-induced coma, the only sign of life she provided were the consistent beeps from the overhead monitor, each of which fueled me to draw my next breath.

Confused, I blinked and then glanced around the room. Sandy's crying woke me from a moment's sleep. I pulled her into my chest and held her tight. Her pain, just as Eddie's had, became mine.

I swept her hair from her face and looked her in the eyes. "Don't cry. She'll wake up soon."

RIGID

"Five minutes," she said through the tears. "If I could have just got there five minutes earlier."

I traced my fingers along the outline of her jaw. "Shhh. I'm proud of you, baby. You saved her life."

She bit into her lip and nodded an ever so slight repeated nod. Then, her eyes fell closed.

Mine soon followed.

Beep.

Beep.

Beep.

THIRTY THREE

Sandy

Eddie wasn't my child, but after what I'd been through, I certainly looked at her no differently than if she were. I'd come to realize in the 36 hours following the events of that night that I wasn't falling in love with Smokey, I loved him.

It may have been slight, and over time I was sure that it might grow, but it was love. I was sure of it.

Everything I wanted in a man, he possessed. It was seeing him as a caring father, however, that seemed to cause me to realize that my love for him was real.

The fact that he was kind, passionate, caring, sexy, humorous, and intelligent mattered, but they were not *all* that mattered. His ability to be an outstanding father was much more important than any of his other qualities.

Smokey folded his arms over his chest. "Let me ask you a question, Doc."

The doctor, man in his early forties, and not the doctor from the previous day, let out a sigh.

Smokey shot him a shitty look. "You bored, Doc?"

"No." He glanced at his watch and then looked up. "You had a question?"

Smokey's eyes narrowed. "You need to be somewhere?"

"I've got…I have several patients that I need to--"

Smokey motioned to the loveseat with his eyes. "Have a seat Doc." He looked at me. "Shut the door, Sandy."

Oh shit.

"I really…I need to--" the doctor stammered.

I pushed the door closed and walked back into the room.

"Have a seat, Doc," Smokey said in a stern tone.

Nervously, the doctor sat down.

Smokey dropped his voice to a calm tone. "Talk to me, Doc. Do you have kids?"

"I do."

"If this was your daughter, what would you do?"

"As parents, we're forced to make decisions for our minor children. The decisions we make--"

"Stop the textbook bullshit, motherfucker. You gave me two options. Keep her on the meds, or take her off them. What would you do? Honest fucking response is all I want. Your daughter is in that bed. You need to make a decision, and you've got five seconds to do it."

"One."

"Two."

"Three."

The doctor cleared his throat. "I'd take her off the medication."

Smokey's head cocked to the side. "Why'd you recommend we leave her on them?"

"It's the safest thing to do, but there are risks inherent to--"

"Stop. If we take her off, what happens?"

"She may wake up. She may not. In the drug-induced state, however, we can only monitor what we *believe* to be her conditions. In this state, one would never *know* the improvements that might be made without the medication. It's simply impossible to tell."

Smokey looked at me.

I shrugged.

"Help me out here, baby."

"I think. She's strong. She's just like you, Smokey. She's a little bitty you. She's a fighter. I say take her off and let her come out of it. I think she'll--"

He looked at the doctor. "Take her off the meds."

"Smokey," I gasped. "I don't want you to do anything--"

"We made this decision, baby. You and me." He shot the doctor a look. "Can we get this done sometime *today*, Doc?"

Smokey's sarcastic tone caused the doctor to jump from his seat. "I'll. We'll get that process underway."

"Thanks Doc."

As the doctor fled the room, Smokey took me in his arms.

I'd made a parental decision, and as much as I wanted it to, it didn't feel good.

In fact, it hurt.

As we stood in each other's arms at the foot of the bed, he began to hum. The dull drone from his chest provided a comfort I hadn't felt in days. I closed my eyes and allowed myself to drift away

Soon, the swaying turned into a slow dance.

It was the slowest of dances, but it was a dance nonetheless.

Eddie's medication stopped, but the dancing continued. Driven by a tune that only Smokey was hearing, we shuffled gracefully across the floor.

RIGID

And, I fell a little further in love with Grayson Wallace.

THIRTY FOUR

Smokey

My eyes shot open.

I glanced around the room, certain *something* had happened.

I could feel my heart beating in my throat.

"Sandy," I whispered. "Wake up."

She opened her eyes. "What happened?"

"I don't know. I thought I heard something."

She looked in either direction, and then at me. "There's nobody here. It was probably a dream."

I looked at the monitor. Everything looked the same. It hadn't changed in three days.

Frustrated, I stood.

"It's late, get some rest," she said.

I shook my head. "I can't sleep. I need a cup of coffee."

Beep.

Beep. Beep.

Beep.

I spun around.

Beep. Beep.

Beep.

Beep. Beep.

RIGID

I rushed to the side of the bed and looked at her.

She opened her eyes, blinked, and then opened them again.

My heart shot to my throat. I rushed to the edge of the bed and took her hand in mine. "I'm here, Lumpy. Daddy's here."

Tears came, flowing down my cheeks like a river. My bottom lip quivered uncontrollably.

"Sandy," I said, my voice nothing more than a gasp for breath. "She's,,,she's awake."

"I'm here," she said from the other side of the bed.

I looked at her and then at Eddie.

With her face still bandaged, and nothing but her swollen eyes, and the tops of her cheeks exposed, she looked like a mummy.

A beautiful mummy.

A tube in her throat prevented her from speaking.

"I…I love…you," I said.

She blinked.

"Eddie? I love you, too," Sandy said.

She blinked again.

As the doctors and nurses rushed in, I reluctantly stepped aside. Sandy rushed to me, and wrapped her arms around me.

Together, we shed a tear.

But this time they were tears of joy.

THIRTY FIVE

Sandy

They had just taken the tubes out of her throat, and although her bandages hadn't changed, she could at least speak. According to the doctors, she would be taken out of ICU by the end of the day. Eager to hear everything she had to say, Smokey and I stood on opposites sides of the bed and waited with baited breath.

He fed her a few more ice chips. "Does it hurt?"

She blinked.

"Can you talk?"

She widened her eyes.

"Maybe," she whispered. "I love…" Her eyes rolled in my direction. She blinked and then looked at Smokey. "Both of you."

"We love you, too."

"I uhhm. I can't remember…"

Smokey looked at me, and then at Eddie. "Don't worry about what happened that night. You need to get better so we can get you out of here."

I hoped she'd never be able to remember what happened. I feared I'd never forget it, but to think of her recalling the events of that night made me feel ill.

"My arm hurts," she whispered.

Smokey sighed. "It's broken."

"That sucks."

"Could be a lot worse."

She blinked a few times, and then looked at the cup of ice. After Smokey gave her a few more ice chips, she continued.

"I want pie. Apple pie."

Smokey laughed. "I'll check with the doctor. Maybe in a few days."

"Someone was. A guy tried to. Where's my ring?" she stammered.

I held up my hand. "Right here, waiting for you to wake up."

She blinked.

Smokey looked up. "Jesus fucking Christ."

I turned toward the door. Dressed in a burgundy set of scrubs and a new pair of tennis shoes, P-Nut sauntered into the room.

"Someone order a sexy nurse?" he asked.

"What in the absolute hell are you doing, Nut?"

"They wouldn't let me up here for three days. Fellas downstairs said she woke up, so I went and bought these. Had to do something."

"You crazy prick." Smokey looked him up and down, and then shook his head. "What's covering your tattoos?"

I hadn't noticed until Smokey said so, but the tattoos that covered P-Nut's forearms were gone.

He peeled a flesh-colored sleeve up his arm and exposed the tattoos. "TatJacket. Got it at the same place."

Smokey shook his head and laughed, honestly out and out laughed, for the first time in days.

P-Nut wedged his way between me and the bed. "What's up, Ed?"

"Just chillin'," she whispered. "You?"

"Same. You've got a pretty big fan group downstairs, kid."

"Do I?"

He nodded. "I don't know. Maybe twenty or thirty. Sometimes more, sometimes less."

She looked at Smokey.

"Don't look at me," he said. "I haven't so much as left this room."

She looked at P-Nut. "Who?"

"Most of the time, Richard's down there. His parents came a few times. Some of Red and White's best. The FFMC. Their Ol' Ladies."

He looked at Smokey. "And, that piece of shit Tank kept comin' by and askin' questions. I told him to kick rocks, and he hasn't been back since."

"Red and White?" she asked.

"Hells Angels."

She nodded.

He looked at Smokey. "That Bama fucker's been here three days."

"He's good people," Smokey said.

"Don't know about that. The fucker kept tryin' to talk to me, so I went and sat by some family that was waiting on grandma to get out of hip surgery for a while. Then, I sat with some sexy bitch while she waited for her husband to get out of heart surgery. Bitch was a MILF, I'm tellin' ya. Pretty much been bored to death waitin'."

P-Nut was weird, but I really liked him. Having everyone together, as strange as it seemed to admit, made me feel like we were a family. The thought of a room filled with people who cared enough about Eddie's welfare to stay and wait for the three days was comforting. It proved just how sincere Smokey's friends were. They were an extension, so to speak, of our immediate family.

While P-Nut talked to Eddie, I held her hand in mine. Within no time, I was daydreaming about living a life that also included the child Smokey and I shared. After getting through the situation we were in, we'd undoubtedly be able to handle anything that life tossed our way.

Anything at all.

THIRTY SIX

Smokey

Eddie was finally home, and short of a few stitches and a cast on her arm, she appeared unchanged. I couldn't help but wonder how the trauma she had been through might affect her, but as she had yet to discuss the events of that night, I had no idea what to expect.

It seemed all she remembered was a man trying to take her ring, and short of asking about it once, that night was never spoken of again.

While Sandy worked her shift at the seafood restaurant, Eddie and I sat at the kitchen table and ate apple pie.

She took a bite of the pie, and then a drink of milk. "It feels good to be home."

"I bet. I can't stand hospitals. Places creep me out."

"I don't think I like them, either."

I admired her for a moment, and then cut a piece of pie with the edge of my fork. "Pie's good. It was nice of Richard's mom to send it."

She looked up. "Do you think you and Sandy will get married?"

Her question caught me off guard. I stared at the pie for a moment, and then looked up. I knew how I felt, but had no idea how Eddie would feel knowing.

One thing I couldn't do, however, was lie to her.

"I think we will, eventually, why?"

She shrugged. "I really like her."

"What would you think if we did?"

She poked her pie a few times, and then looked at me. "I'd like it."

"Would you?"

Her eyes lost focus and she gave a slow nod. "Yeah. I would."

While I fidgeted with my pie, my questions about that night were answered.

"I uhhm. He came up behind me, and grabbed my shoulder," she said, her voice without emotion.

I looked at her. Seeing her go through the hell of reliving that night would kill me. "Eddie, I don't think it's a good idea--"

"I'm okay. Let me tell you what happened."

I wanted to know, I just didn't want her to tell me.

"Are you sure?" I asked.

"Yeah. I've been thinking about it a lot."

I let out a sigh and pushed myself away from the table. "Okay."

Her eyes dropped to the table. "He asked for my ring, and I told him no. Then, he grabbed my arm. I uhhm. I hit him a few times, but it's different. It's not like *kyorugi* or *shihap*."

She let out a sigh and looked up. "He uhhm. He hit me in the face and knocked me down--"

"Ed…"

She raised her good hand. "Let me talk."

It hurt to hear it, but if she needed to rid herself of the memories, I needed to let her.

"Okay."

"He kept trying to take it, and I poked my thumbs in his eyes, you know, like you taught me."

I grinned and nodded. "Good for you."

"He uhhm. So, he was hitting me and stuff, and I screamed for Sandy. And then I blacked out or something. It gets weird after that. But then, I heard her."

"Sandy?"

"Uh huh."

She began to poke her pie with her fork. "She uhhm. She screamed. I remember that. She uhhm. She said…"

She inhaled a long breath and looked up. "Hey mother effer. Get off my daughter."

I chuckled and cried at the same time. I quickly wiped my eyes and looked at her. "She said mother effer?"

She shook her head. "She said the other one. She screamed it."

I hoped it was all she remembered.

"Is that all you remember?"

She shook her head. "I remember the sound of the gun. And then of her pulling him off of. She uhhm. She pulled him off me. And she talked to me. She called me *my baby*. And she said she loved me." She met my gaze. "You call me baby."

My throat tightened.

I swallowed hard and I nodded. "Yeah, I do."

"I remember the ambulance guys. They were talking on the way to the hospital. Said the guy was dead. She shot him in the head."

"Eddie, it's not anything that needs to be--"

"I'm glad she shot him, dad. I hate to say it, but I really am." She huffed a sigh and raised her cast. "Look at me. I mean, really. Yeah, he needed to be shot."

I couldn't agree with her more, but refrained from giving an opinion.

RIGID

"I'm just glad it's over," I said.

She smashed her pie with the tines of her fork, and after flattening it into a pile, she looked up and nodded. "Yeah, me too."

I pushed my plate to the side.

Two months prior, marrying Sandy was unthinkable. Now, it was all I could think about. It had very little to do with Eddie's question, though. I desperately wanted to do everything right, be married, have a family, and raise our baby in as conventional of an atmosphere as a 1%er and a former stripper could.

I looked at Eddie. "What if it was sooner, rather than later?"

"What if what was sooner?"

"Sandy and I getting married."

She smiled. "Far as I'm concerned, the sooner the better."

THIRTY SEVEN

Sandy

Eddie and Richard were on a date, and Smokey and I were on pins and needles since she'd left. While Smokey went to the bathroom for what seemed like the tenth time of the night, I sat and listened to the music.

The doorbell buzzing caused me to jump from my seat.

"Get that, will ya?" Smokey shouted from the bathroom. "Probably Cholo dropping off a check."

I walked to the door, opened it, and gawked at who stood on the porch. He was dressed differently than he was at the police station, but I'd never forget his face.

Detective Watson.

My throat constricted and my mouth went dry. "Do you. Do you have a uhhm. A search warrant?"

He blinked and then coughed a laugh. "Excuse me?"

"If you don't have a search warrant, you can't come in. House rules."

"I need to talk to your significant other," he said.

"Sorry. No can do."

"I think he'll want to hear what I have to say, and I do believe you owe me a favor."

I heard the bathroom door open and then close.

"Smokey, the cops are here."

RIGID

"What?"

Smokey stepped between me and the door, and looked at Watson. "You lost?"

Watson shook his head. "Need to talk to you for a moment."

"Concerning what?"

He glanced over each shoulder, and then met Smokey's hardened gaze. "May I come in?"

"Afraid not."

He looked at me. "I saved your ass, and you know it. All I need is five minutes."

"What's he talking about? Smokey asked.

"He uhhm. He's the one that got me the attorney."

"Sounds like a cop move," Smokey said. "Save the girl to get to the Ol' Man?"

Watson shook his head, and then rolled up the edge of his shirt sleeve. He turned his muscular bicep toward us and revealed a tattoo.

He cocked an eyebrow. "Look familiar?"

Smokey studied the tattoo, and then nodded. "Might have seen one like that before."

"What is it?" I asked.

"Navy SEAL," Smokey said. He looked at Watson. "You want a fucking cookie?"

"Sorry, just had a donut. I'm full." Watson said, stone-faced. He cocked his head to the side. "Let's say I'm looking out for your President's best interest."

"Go talk to him," Smokey said. "Time for me to shut the door."

Watson chuckled a dry laugh. "He's a prick. And it's not him I'm worried about right now, it's *you*."

264

"Afraid I can't help you," Smokey said.

Watson shrugged. "Guess you won't mind doing a twenty-year bit in club fed? By the time you get out, your daughter will be five years older than you are now."

Smokey spit out a laugh. "Haven't done anything. And, I don't scare easy. Go pull someone else's cock, cop."

"At the hamburger joint off Highway 8." Watson cleared his throat and then widened his eyes a little. "The guy at your bike? The fight that special agent Brickman got into? It was a set-up. Your prospect, Tank? He's a special agent with the ATF. Name's Brickman. The other guy was an ATF underling."

Smokey's face went stark white.

He pulled the door open. "Come on in."

THIRTY EIGHT

Smokey

I paced back and forth in P-Nut's garage, debating on exactly what I needed to say. I was convinced I needed to say nothing, but I knew resolving the situation on my own was impossible.

"What in the fuck, Brother?" P-Nut asked. "When was the last time you came by at 1:00 in the fucking morning? Hell, you never come *here*."

"Just give me a minute."

Sitting on the steps that led to his house, he took a drag off his cigarette. "Ed's okay, ain't she?"

I paused and turned toward him. "Yeah."

He blew the smoke down at his feet and then looked up. "Sandy okay?"

"Yep."

I started pacing again.

"New baby healthy?"

I nodded. "Yeah."

"Smoke, you're making me *itch*." He stood, scratched his forearm, and let out a half-assed growl. "What the fuck's going on?"

I stopped, took a long breath, and then looked up at the ceiling. "Shut the garage door."

Concern covered his face. He stood, pushed the wall-mounted button, and the garage door closed.

I looked at him and let out a sigh. "Tank. The prospect?"

He nodded. "What about him?"

"He's a federal agent. ATF. His name's Special Agent Brickman. He was investigating Meathead for a *felon in possession* tip that the ATF got from one of the Savages, and after he busted Meat, he just kind of fell into my lap."

He started scratching his head. "I fucking *knew* it. Cocksucker." He looked at me with crazy eyes. "How you want me to take care of it?"

"We need to think. Make a plan."

He pressed his hands to his hops and shot me a glare. After a long pause, he shook his head. "You're fucking scared."

"That's not it."

"Face your fears," he said. "You say that shit all the time. *Face your fears*. If you're scared, just say it."

"That's not the case."

"The Smoke I been knowin' would be on the road right now, ready to whack this cat into pieces with a hatchet. Something's stoppin' you."

I stood and stared, not quite sure if he was right, or if I simply needed to make a plan.

He looked at me with narrow eyes. "How'd you find out?"

"Got a tip from an outsider. Checks out, though. Even saw pictures of him from the academy and all his credentials. It's legit."

He nodded. "All I need to know."

I considered what he said. Taking care of the situation without a plan would be a recipe for disaster. "We can't just *do it*. We've gotta watch our backs. And, we need to give it some thought. Serious thought. If we just kill this prick, they'll come for us. We need to make it look like something else. Fuck, I don't know. Set it up and make it look like an accident."

"*We* ain't doing shit, Smoke. I'll take care of that cocksucker."

I shook my head. "He's not your problem," I said. "He's mine."

"Beg to differ with you, Brother. Your problems *are* my problems."

"Not this time."

He crossed his arms, and looked me up and down. "This time more than any other time, motherfucker."

"Just take it easy. We need to think about this. Last thing I need is this prick setting me up on a crime."

"That's what I'm talking about. You got Eddie, Sandy, a new baby coming. Shit, Brother. Last thing you need is some rotten fed planting a hot piece in your bags or putting a kilo of crank in your house. Rotten pricks. I'll take care of this."

"*We'll* take care of it."

"Okay. Sounds great. Draft up a plan, and have your people get with my people. We'll do lunch and decide when we can get it scheduled," he said, his voice thick with sarcasm.

"What are you saying?"

"Nothing." He shrugged. "We'll figure something out."

"I'm serious, Nut. I came here to get your opinion. The last thing I need is you going solo on this deal, and end up doing something stupid."

He shot me a look. "Now I'm a dumbass, huh?"

"Didn't say that."

"You think all I do is dumb shit?"

"Didn't say that, either."

"I'm smarter than you give me credit."

"You're the most solid fucker I know, Nut." I let out a heavy sigh and looked right at him. "But you're fucking nuts."

"No shit," he said with a laugh. "Tell me something I don't know."

"We need to give this some serious thought."

"Go home and get some rest," he said. "We'll talk about it tomorrow."

I was exhausted. He was right. I needed to get some rest, wake up fresh, and think about it. "My mind's going a hundred miles an hour right now."

"Mine too. Get some rest, Brother. Think about it. We'll talk about it tomorrow."

I nodded. "Nervous as fuck, Brother."

"Makes two of us. Glad you found out, though."

"Makes two of us."

"I'm gonna hit the rack," he said. "Too much for one night. I'm itching all over."

"I'll head out."

"Shiny side up," he said.

"I'll do my best." I turned toward the door. "Open the door?"

He pressed the button. "Give them gals a hug for me, would ya?"

I glanced over my shoulder. "Will do."

I tossed and turned all night, getting very little sleep at all. It bothered me that Nut thought I was *scared*.

By the time morning arrived, I decided he was right. Not completely, but partially.

I feared losing everything that I had spent a lifetime unknowingly searching for.

THIRTY NINE

Sandy

Eddie finished chewing her food and set her hamburger down. "So, what did the doctor say? You went to the doctor today, right?"

"Oh, yeah." I alternated glances between her and Smokey. "Everything looks good. It's a kumquat baby. That's what she said. Bigger than a grape, but not as big as a little bitty lime. It's got lungs and a brain and everything. It's just hard to believe. It's exciting."

"The baby's healthy? You're healthy?" Smokey asked.

"Yep. Good for another four weeks. She said no more stress, though."

"Hopefully all that's behind us."

It had been two weeks since detective Watson stopped by, and not one word had been mentioned about the matter since. The one time I had asked, his response was that it was *nothing to worry about.*

I had no idea if it was nothing to worry about, or something I simply needed to try and forget. Either way, I wasn't concerned. I trusted Smokey to keep Eddie and me safe from all the things that threatened to split us apart.

"I'm sure it is," I said.

"That's exciting," Eddie said. "It's weird to think about, though. A kumquat. That's crazy."

I took the last bite of my hamburger. "Mmhhmm."

"Damn," Smoky said. "You're done already?"

"I was starving."

Eddie slid the platter across the table. "Eat. You've got to feed the baby." She pointed toward the hamburgers. "Maybe it's twins."

"Oh, don't say that," I said. "I can't even…"

"That would be awesome," Smokey said. "Twins?"

"I know, right?" Eddie chimed.

"Wait." I looked at them both. "Neither of you are carrying them, giving birth to them, or breastfeeding them. Twins would be insane."

Eddie shot Smokey an excited look. "Insane and freaking awesome."

I grabbed another burger and shook my head. "No twins."

"Did you tell her?" Eddie asked.

Smokey shook his head lightly, as if trying to dismiss her question. "What?"

He raised both eyebrows and shook his head.

I looked at Eddie. "What?"

She looked at Smokey.

I scowled at each of them. "What?"

"I had a dream," Smokey said.

I took a bite of my new burger. "And?"

He shrugged. "Twins."

I took another bite. "So."

"Sometimes his dreams come true," Eddie said.

"What?" My eyes shot to Smokey. "Really?"

"I don't know. There's been a few that were questionable. Nothing to worry about."

I took another bite of my burger, swallowed it, and then studied him. "Are you serious?"

"About the dream, or about worrying about it?"

"About the dream."

He nodded. "I had a dream the other day. A boy, and a girl. Twins."

I sighed. "I sure hope not."

"I sure hope *so*," Eddie said.

"So do I," Smokey agreed.

He motioned toward my plate and laughed. "Want another?"

I looked down.

My plate was void of any food.

I hadn't realized it, but I'd eaten the other burger already. "Holy crap," I gasped. "I can't believe it."

They looked at each other and chuckled.

"It's not twins," I said.

"Still hungry?" Smokey asked.

I shrugged. "Not really."

I was, though.

"Are you sure?" Eddie asked.

"Yeah," I said. "I'm okay."

She picked up her burger, and took a bite. "This is so good," she said over her mouthful of food. "Better than *In-N-Out*."

Smokey took a bite. "It's cooked just right, too. Great job, Ed."

"Thanks." She took another bite and then looked at me, and shook her head in disbelief. "Mmmm."

I looked at the platter.

There were four left.

I reached for one. "Maybe half."

I took a bite.

It tasted *so* good.

RIGID

Smokey stood, opened the refrigerator door, and pulled out the horseradish sauce. "Here."

I pulled the top half of the bun off, covered the top with sauce, and took a bite.

Oh my God.

I was in heaven.

I took a bite, and then another. Before I knew it, the burger was gone and I was licking my fingers.

"Three down." Eddie nodded her head toward the platter. "Three to go."

I shook my head. "I'm done." I patted my stomach. "I'm stuffed."

"When we get done with dinner, I've got ice cream and brownies," Eddie said. "But you're probably not hungry, are you?"

"You got ice cream?"

She nodded. "Neapolitan, and Rocky Road."

I shrugged. "I don't know. Maybe a little brownie, and like a tiny scoop. Not much, though."

Smokey and Eddie looked at each other and did the high-five thing.

I rolled my eyes.

Twins.

The thought of it was the most ridiculous thing ever.

That night at midnight, when I was sneaking another burger and eating ice cream with a fork, I began to wonder.

As I sat on the floor with a burger in one hand, and the tub of ice cream between my legs, Eddie snuck in behind me.

"Boo!" she whispered.

I all but jumped out of my pajamas.

She sat down beside me and took the fork from my hand. "Still thinking it's only one?"

With a mouthful of burger, I looked at her and nodded.

She poked the fork into the ice cream and then looked at me. "You've almost killed this."

With my mouth still full, I responded. "I know."

She shook her head and laughed. "Either way, I'm really excited."

I took another bite. "Me, too."

After digging around in the tub for a minute, she managed to excavate another bite from the matter stuck to the edges.

She poked the fork in her mouth and placed the empty container between my legs. She nodded toward my burger. "I won't tell if you won't tell."

I raised my hand. "Girl power."

She slapped her hand against mine. "Girl Power."

I poked the last part of the burger in my mouth and savored every morsel of it, closing my eyes as I chewed.

"What in the fuck are you two doing?" Smokey snarled from behind us.

We both jumped, me so high, the cardboard ice cream container shot from between my legs and slid across the tile floor.

I spun around, swallowed my food, and shrugged one shoulder.

He glanced at the empty platter, and then looked at the ice cream tub. "Well?"

There was no sense in lying, so I told him the absolute truth.

"What do you think," I said with a shrug. "I'm feeding the twins."

FORTY

Smokey

It had been a month since Tank came up missing, but there were no missing person's reports, no nosey ATF agents poking around, and no arrests. Convinced the investigation was over, and he simply went to harass someone else, I exhaled and began to live my life the way I saw fit.

P-Nut was right.

I was scared.

Not of Tank, or of the thought of resolving the issue with him.

But I did fear two things.

Snakes, and making the commitment to marry. As easy as it was to come to terms mentally with the thought of doing it, and as much as I wanted a family, I simply couldn't develop the courage to ask Sandy any more than I could pick up a snake.

So, I decided to do what it was that I spent a lifetime suggesting others do.

Face my fears.

"Be a badass piece when we're done," he said.

I looked down at my chest. "Got three solid days in right now. Been tough to hide this fucker."

The tattoo artist stopped. "Hide it?"

RIGID

I nodded. "It's a surprise."

"How the fuck you hide a full chest piece?"

"It isn't easy, believe me."

He positioned the needle over my stomach. "Ready?"

I clenched my jaw. "Go."

The needle, a four-pronged shading rig, dug into my flesh.

The blue ink of the snake's belly was an aqua color, and reminded me of the ocean. It was the one place I could always find solace, regardless of what was going on in my life.

As the needle tore away at my tanned skin, and replaced it with a permanent ink, I felt like I was gaining one thing, and losing another.

The artist drilled into my skin until the needle ran dry of the ink, and then he'd dip it in the well, and start the process again. The pain was almost intolerable, but I wouldn't give up for any reason, I knew that much.

What I gained from the completed tattoo would last a lifetime.

With each drop of ink, my fear was slowly rising from my soul, leaving me feeling cleansed.

I gained a torso covered with my greatest fear.

A snake.

I would never again fear the most repulsive creature created by God. In fact, it would become part of my very being. I wasn't facing my fear, I was embracing it.

I was becoming it.

The pain shot through me like an electric shock. Every muscle in my body tensed. The third of three solid days of tattooing, and my skin resembled hamburger.

But, it was the only way.

I closed my eyes, took my mind to thoughts of raising another child, and of Sandy and I walking along the beach with all our children at our side. Playing in the waves, and finding seashells, we'd walk the coastline for hours to find the perfect spot to set up for the day.

If our baby was a boy, he would grow up to love the ocean, respect, it, and probably be a surfer.

If our baby was a girl, she'd grow up to be just like Eddie. Strong, resilient, and bold.

"Have a look, Boss," he said.

I opened my eyes. "You done."

He wiped a towel across my stomach. "I think that's it. Never seen that before."

"What's that?" I asked.

"Fucker falling asleep when he was getting drilled on the chest."

I shot him a look. "What time is it?"

He glanced at the clock. "4:00."

Somehow, I'd lost four hours. I slipped off the side of the chair, turned toward the mirror, and looked at my reflection.

The snake started at my belt, and ran all the way to the top of my chest. According to the artist, the design was a Chinese theme, and was considered a symbol of healing, rebirth, renewal, and protection.

It may have all been in my head, but I felt different already. I was sure of it. I nodded at my reflection. "Fucker's perfect."

"Appreciate it."

He cleaned the tattoo, covered my torso in plastic wrap, and then I put on my shirt.

"Can I leave this shit on for, say, an hour or so?"

"No problem. When you remove it, be sure and wash the plasma off.

RIGID

You've got plenty of ink, you know the drill."

"Just got one more stop to make," I said.

"Where you headed?"

"Exit 3B off the 8. Friars."

He nodded, but I doubt he knew where I was going. "Gotcha."

I walked through the door, and looked up at the cloudless sky. It was a beautiful day to be a new man – a man who faced his fears – and that was exactly what I was.

A new man.

Who was fearless.

FORTY ONE

Sandy

Smokey, Eddie and I were going to dinner at a nice restaurant in San Diego with Cholo and Lex. I was so excited to be enjoying an evening with another couple, and spending time with a friend who was only a few weeks more pregnant than me was a lot of fun.

Lex and I compared our belly size, our moods, doctor's recommendations, and even our likes and dislikes with food.

I stared down at my belly as the water sprayed against me. Now at 13 weeks, I was starting to show. Seeing the growth was the best part of the pregnancy so far.

Eddie bought some board books, and gave them to us as a gift. When we were in bed, Smokey read them to the baby, often creating additional bits and pieces as he saw fit, and making the story his own. He said the reading sessions would cause the baby to get used to his raspy voice.

That way there would be no surprises after the birth.

Living with Smokey and Eddie was, by far the highlight of my life. Part of me had an expectation that one day it would all end, because it was simply too good to be true. The thought of *not* having it was extremely unhealthy for me, and I knew it.

So, when those thoughts came, I'd always talk to Eddie, and she would tell me how much I meant to her, and to her father. She explained that it was difficult for Smokey to express how he felt, because he, too, feared losing me.

In the end, it seemed Grayson and I were far more alike than I originally thought.

Two people who met, got pregnant, and then, at least one of them fell in love. It was a fairy tale if there ever was one, but it was put together with our timeline, not one from most fables.

It was *my* happy ever after.

And, I wouldn't have it any other way.

I got out of the shower, dried off, and put on my robe. When I came out of the bedroom, I about had a heart attack.

A real one.

"Oh my God!" I shouted. "What…"

I stood and stared.

Against the far wall, Smokey stood, shirtless, wearing only jeans. From his chest, all the way down to his crotch, a huge colorful snake was tattooed.

It was one of the sexiest things I'd ever seen. In fact, it sucked the breath from my lungs, leaving it difficult for me to breathe.

"What. Oh my God. What. I thought you hated snakes?" I stammered.

"Do you like it?"

I sucked in a breath. "Uhhm. It's. yeah. I like it. It's uhhm. It's super hot. I uhhm, Dear God. I though nothing could make you hotter. But. Uhhm. Yeah."

He cocked his head to the side. "Do you think it's sexy?"

"Uhhm. Yeah. Like. I wanna fuck you right now."

"Ahem," a voice said from my left.

I glanced to my side. Eddie was sitting on the side of the bed.

What the fuck?

I was embarrassed, but more than anything, I was shocked that she was sitting on our bed. The entire ordeal seemed weird, but I dismissed it to her probably admiring Smokey's new tattoo.

"What are you...I uhhm." I shrugged innocently. "Sorry."

"It's okay." She grinned. "I like it too. Just not quite as much as you, obviously."

I looked at Smokey, swallowed, and then let out a sigh. "I uhhm. I need to get dressed. And if you want that to happen, you're both going to have to go somewhere else."

He shook his head. "Two things. First of all, since when do I leave when you get dressed?"

"Since you got that tattoo," I said. "If you stay, we bone. If we bone, we'll be late. So, you gotta go, mister."

I looked at Eddie and cocked my head to the side. "Sorry Eddie."

She raised her eyebrows. "No big deal."

I looked at Smokey. "What's the second thing?"

"Neither of us are going *anywhere*," he said.

I wrinkled my brow. "Huh? I've got to get ready."

He pushed himself from the wall, walked up to me, and looked me over. "We need to talk to you."

The tone of his voice was different. It wasn't angry, but it wasn't happy, either. I scanned my memory for anything I might have done, and short of eating the rest of the hot dogs, came up with nothing.

"Both of you?"

He nodded.

"Okay."

"We have a question," Eddie said.

I looked at her. "Uhhm. Okay."

She looked at Smokey. "You first, or me?"

He shrugged.

I looked at her.

She met my gaze, let out a sigh, and scratched her nose with her cast. "I need to know something," she said dryly.

I cinched my robe. "Okay."

"So do I," Smokey said.

Eddie cleared her throat. "Me first."

"No, me first," Smokey insisted.

Eddie looked at Smokey. "At the same time?"

He cocked his head to the side. "Sounds good."

"On three?" she asked.

"I like four better," he said.

I was lost. And scared. They were acting weird, and neither of them seemed overly happy.

Smokey lifted my chin until my eyes met his. "Pay attention," he demanded.

"I'm trying to," I said.

Eddie hopped off the edge of the bed and stepped beside Smokey.

"Ready?" he asked.

She nodded and slipped her arm around him.

Simultaneously, they spoke. "One."

"Two."

"Three."

"Four."

Smokey's eyes widened. "I love you with all my heart. Will you marry me?"

Eddie grinned. "Will you be my mom?"

My face went flush. I stumbled, and almost fell, but Smokey caught me.

I looked at Eddie.

A tear rolled down her cheek. "Please?"

I nodded eagerly. "I uhhm." I looked at Smokey and wiped my cheek. My dream was now a reality. "Yes, I'd love to be your wife."

I looked at Eddie and opened my arms. "And, yes. I'd be honored to be your mother."

The three of us embraced in a hug.

After a long embrace, Eddie leaned away, reached inside her cast, and pulled something out. "You almost forgot this, dork."

Smokey coughed out a laugh and reached for her hand. "Sorry, it's my first time."

He lowered himself to one knee. "Sandy, know this first. I love you dearly. If you'll honor me in being my wife, I'd like to give you this ring, as a token of my promise to you to be your husband."

I truly loved them both will all my heart. Although my initial belief was that things needed to happen in a particular order, I now realized there wasn't a recipe when it came to love. Love simply either happened or it didn't.

For us, it did.

"I will," I said.

After those two spoken words, he slipped the ring on my finger.

And, my fairy tale was complete.

Well, almost.

EPILOGUE

Eddie

We're provided opportunities through our experiences. What we choose to pay attention to and what we choose to dismiss determine how our lives unfold.

That's what I think, anyway.

What do I know? I'm just a seventeen-year-old girl.

Wish I had a piece of apple pie for every time I heard that one.

Seventeen, going on forty is more like it.

My experiences in life molded me into who I am, therefore I have no regrets. Not one. My pinky finger will never bend again, and every time I look at it, it stands as a reminder of the night I was attacked.

I wouldn't erase that night if I could roll back the clock, though.

It was on *that* night that I decided that my mom was pretty special. It wasn't because she saved me, or that she shot the guy who was sure to kill me if she'd been absent from my life. It was what she said in a time of desperation.

When she thought the least, and acted out of a mother's God-given nature.

She called me her daughter.

My heart melted that night. But not as much as it did the day in the hospital.

287

Sit down for a minute, and I'll tell you how it all unfolded.

We had an appointment to get the first ultrasound. I say *we* because the three of us went. Mom was excited, but not as much as dad and me. They wouldn't let P-Nut come into the room, because he ended up trying to mack on a nurse, and then things went downhill fast.

Well, that, and he was acting like P-Nut. He's a hard man to understand. Not so much for me, but for everyone else.

Anyway.

The doctor put the gel on mom's tummy, and started the scan. Dad and I had our eyes glued to the screen, and mom's mouth went a mile a minute. That's sixty miles an hour, if you do the math.

"So, you can tell for sure?" mom asked.

The doctor pressed the device to her stomach. "Can you hold still?"

She reached for dad's hand. "I'm sorry."

Dad's eyes stayed fixed on the monitor.

"Okay," the doctor said. "You wanted to know sex, is that correct?"

The three of us said *yes* at the same time.

The doctor clicked a button and froze the screen. It looked like a jumbled up mess until she pointed to everything with her mouse.

She moved the pointer. "These are the hips."

She moved it again, "This is the left foot."

She slid it over a little more. "And this is the penis."

"It's a boy?" mom gasped.

The doctor nodded. "Yes, *this* is a boy."

Her and dad oohed and aahed, but I said very little, other than smiling.

The doctor pushed another button, and went back to a live feed. After a moment, she stopped the screen again.

"These are the hips."

"This is the nose."

"And, this is the vagina."

I jumped from my seat, knocking the stool across the room. "Fuck Yes!"

The doctor damned near fell from her stool. I turned toward dad and raised my hand in the air.

He slapped his hand against mine. "I'll pay you later."

"Oh," the doctor said. "Did you have a bet about twins?"

I shook my head. "No. We knew it would be twins. I bet one of them would be a girl."

I'd never been so excited in my entire life.

Not once.

My life was complete. I always had an awesome dad, and I was aware of that.

But, ever since I was a little girl, all I ever wanted was a sister, and a mom.

And, now I had both.

I was so excited, I didn't realize mom was crying. Heck, I was, too. I wiped my tears on my sleeve, leaned over her, and wiped the tears from her cheeks.

"I'm so happy right now," I said excitedly. "I need a milkshake."

She bit into her lip and nodded. Then, she raised her hand high in the air.

"Girl power," she murmured.

She was the best mom ever.

I slapped my hand against hers, and mouthed my mantra.

Girl power.